This one is for all my frien_ these stories with years of great times and those who continue to meet and live on, in the realms.

As well as all my readers and fans that support me in this endeavor and keep asking for more. To the new readers that may become fans and share in the enjoyment of Coeur D'Alene, a very heartfelt:

WELL MET.

CHAPTER 1

The Tigard Valley was marshy to say the least. Namsilat had taken a wrong turn after crossing the Willamette coming out of the SilverLeaf Valley and for three long wet, muddy, insect-infested days they had wandered the 'Swamp'. At mid-day they stopped beside a small pond, as a pair of mallards floated peacefully along a small canal connecting it to the rest of the marsh.

"Look at them, Clifford nothing to do all day but swim and squawk. If they wanted to, they could just take wing and fly right out of here, must be nice." The two and a half year old, three hundred and fifty pound Dire wolf pup turned his eyes from the drifting snacks to his companion, an all too familiar look of inquiry on his face. Even his fire-red eyes looked famished.

"I know what you're thinking 'Mid-day meal', right?" The creature had learned those words early on and upon hearing them he went into his feeding dance. The hair on his tail fluffed up like a frightened cat, wagging back and forth as he followed closely behind his benefactor, racing circles around him, drooling and lapping as Namsilat continued his rant.

"Yeah, I know. You're as bad as Beldoff ever was." Namsilat rebuked as he retrieved a chunk of the elk meat Airapal had suggested he take along 'just in case'. It had only been a week since they parted and he already missed her.

"I have an obligation to my people." Probably not the most original dismissal, but a first for him he reflected as he tossed the huge chunk of dried flesh to the waiting hound.

"Okay, okay. I'll feed you next, but despite your ornery side, you're not likely to see me as a substitute for a missed meal." He spoke to Lester as he made his way to the grain sack.

In two chomps, Clifford devoured half the hunk of elk Namsilat had given him. He threw his head back and smacked down in one very loud crunch, finishing a five pound slab of dried meat, his long rough tongue circling his entire face as he fixed his eyes on his provider. "You're going to get fat eating like that, and don't think you're getting any of my meal." Namsilat sat down against the trunk of a small maple tree along the bank of the pond. He could feel the burning eyes of Clifford as he bit into his jerky.

"Mmmph." He could swear he heard the Dire wolf whimper.

"Are you kidding me? Did you just beg?" Namsilat did all he could not to laugh, but the thought of a ferocious beast such as a Dire wolf whimpering for food from a simple half-Elf was laughable. He took another bite, and this time the pup belly crawled towards him. After all, Clifford was a wild animal. Airapal told him never to forget that. Also, to never underestimate that he is extremely intelligent.

"If you can keep those two things always in the front of your mind when dealing with him, you should live long enough for him to get tired of hanging around you and he'll leave." Her parting warning before she kissed him.

"Women, always trying to get ya to change your mind." Namsilat was beginning to mumble. He began gazing around the wasteland that was home to the Halfling race. Looking at the swampy marshland, berry briars and ivy, he could not imagine what they saw here. It's wet, smelly and full of unfriendly creatures that either bite you or get in everything you own…hmmm, much like Halflings, he mused.

Everywhere he looked, the water was murky, with skimpy, useless fan-leaf trees. No Pine, Fir or other evergreens. "Give me the mountains." He grumbled.

Namsilat spotted a huge stand of Birch trees some fifty yards across the swamp from where they sat. He hated Birch trees, them and Ironwood. When he was younger, his mother and he depended on the charity of others for many things, fire wood being one of them. The townspeople provided them with lots of Birch and Ironwood. As a boy, he could never understand why grown, experienced men couldn't figure out those two woods were better left where ya found them. But when he was a little older, and the local kids cared less about hurting the young half-Elf's feelings, they began to poke fun at him, telling him how stupid he was for even trying to split the useless wood their dads had given them. That was when he learned to fall trees for himself, and got really good at it. He never did know why so many people hated his race, but he had plenty of reasons for hating most of theirs.

Clifford's growl brought him out of his meanderings and he heard a muffled splash out in the pond. The Dire stood and walked towards the edge of the water as Namsilat looked over the water. Ripples ran out several feet off shore where the pair of ducks had just been moments before.

"You've never seen ducks dive for food Cliffy?" he asked as he reached out, patting the huge creature to offer comfort. Instead of relaxing and returning to begging as was his nature, the fur on the wolf's back raised, as did the hair around his neck, forming a thick red mane. His lips rolled back exposing his teeth and Namsilat realized the creature knew something he didn't. Suddenly FireClaw's Talon, the magical weapon he had taken off the kindred, appeared in his right hand as he leapt to his feet. Lester neighed and began backing away from the water's edge. Clifford's head darted to the left. Namsilat's eyes followed. More ripples, but these seemed to be moving along the ponds edge, towards the trio.

"What is it Clifford?" Just as he broke the silence, a huge blue-grey reptilian head sprang from the water. Swamp grass hung from its lower jaw, and razor-sharp fangs several inches long protruded from its upper jaw as it rose from the murky waters. The slimy water mixed with mud from the shallow pond splashed loudly as it fell from the beasts open maw. As quickly as it appeared, it fell back beneath the dark water. Within seconds the water was calm, giving no indication where the creature had gone.

"Back up Cliff…" was all he got out before the second head emerged, this one directly in front of him and coming straight ahead with wide open mouth and fangs. Clifford growled getting its attention as Namsilat set his footing preparing for the attack. The huge wolf lunged forward, jaw snapping as it bit at the bobbing head, now standing a good five feet out of the water. Not the least bit intimidated by the young wolf, the Hydra flicked its tongue as it made its first strike. Just as it thought it had made good the attack, the magical blade sliced through its exposed neck, causing it to retract, its blood spewing everywhere as it turned its attention back to Namsilat.

"Great Clifford, but don't do anything foolish. I have a feeling this thing has friends…maybe four or five of them." Namsilat brought FireClaw's Talon up to guard as he focused on the head now staring him down. Clifford moved to assist him and just as he stepped into the muck the second head took a strike at him, its huge mouth coming down across the large wolf's furry mane. But chomping down it got nothing but hair. Before it could retract, Clifford's head swung around, his powerful jaws snapping at the head, catching the beast's lower jaw and ripping it completely off. The head Namsilat was facing let out a deafening howl. Clifford shook his head, fighting off the shriek, tossing the hunk of flesh into the water and turning back to the first head.

Ten feet from shore a third head shot out of the sludge, racing across the top of the water as it closed on the Dire wolf. Namsilat barely had time to react. He broke from the first head and raced towards the charging creature, as the largest of the three heads struck out, coming downward towards the side of the Dire wolf. Namsilat thrust his arm up into the throat of the creature, forcing the tip of the blade through its lower jaw, up through its mouth and out the beast's nose right between its eyes.

In death's grip it thrashed, tossing Namsilat with it, splashing him in and out of the muddy water. His mouth filled with slime and the stench made him gag while he tried helplessly to withdraw the blade that was wedged in the creatures withering head. Finally it fell limp on top of him, holding his head just inches under the murky liquid, its blood running out making the water even more distasteful as Namsilat fought to retrieve his sword.

The remaining head turned to strike the helpless fighter. As it did, Clifford pounced, jaws wide open, his mouth clamping down around its throat. The creature was in trouble and it knew it, trying in vain to reach around and bite the clinging wolf. Clifford tightened his bite, snapping several of the beast vertebrates; they hit the water in a huge splash, landing right on top of Namsilat. Namsilat had had enough. Releasing FireClaw's Talon he pushed out from under the huge wolf and its prey and sloshed his way back to shore, falling face first on the muddy bank. Clifford held the creature until he was certain life had left it. Releasing it he returned to the shore. Standing right next to Namsilat he began to twitch a little.

"Do not even think about it…" As he uttered his warning the large hound shook violently, throwing more muddy water on the already drenched Namsilat. "I have got to teach you not to do that." The creature looked him in the eyes and he could hear Airapal's voice. "Good luck with that."

Namsilat lay there for several minutes, drained and soaked. When he sat up on his knees he realized Lester was nowhere to be seen. "Now where did that cowardly horse run off to?" Without thinking he placed his mud covered fingers in his mouth and tried to whistle, spitting out the filth as he cursed. "Damn it Lester, come here. The damn thing is dead, Lester."

He called several more times before becoming concerned. He was trying to train Clifford when it was time to run as opposed to fight, but Lester had learned that lesson all on his own. He never went far however and would usually return to Namsilat's calling. He wiped off his fingers and whistled…still nothing. He called the

Talon and stood, and then walking off in the direction of the horses hoof prints, Clifford fell in behind him. They had only walked about fifty yards when they spotted Lester standing calmly next to a small maple tree. Clifford started out for him, but Namsilat grabbed his neck.

"Easy. Ol' Lester might make me walk sometimes Cliffy, but I have never seen him tie himself to a branch." Namsilat noticed Lester's reins were wrapped around the lowest branch of the small tree. He looked around, and then let Clifford go ahead of him. There were very few things known to live in the swamp that would confront a Dire wolf, and Namsilat hadn't seen any Giant tracks so he figured it was safe. The huge pup ran out and began shaking off more of the muddy water, coating Namsilat's ride in the slime as well. "You know, you'll get yours Clifford." Namsilat yelled as he approached.

"So, Lester my friend, when did you learn to tie yourself off you been keepin' secrets from Ol' Namsilat?" Scanning the area with his infra vision, Namsilat made certain they weren't being watched. He tossed himself up on Lester and turned the horse back toward their camp to gather the remaining gear before heading out.

He had enjoyed just about all of this swamp he could.

CHAPTER 2

"I have a feeling, Cliffy old boy, that we might have been doubled back on. Why don't you run ahead and say hello to whoever might be ransacking our gear." With that the huge creature took off in a dead run, breaking through the underbrush and crashing like a herd of elk.

Up ahead, several yards Namsilat heard desperate screams from what sounded like children. Fearing what he had done he spurred Lester. Not something the horse cared for; he jerked hard, threw his head down and barreled through the brush. Once on the other side and feeling Namsilat's body relax ever so slightly, the horse reaffirmed his disapproval, locking up his body and tossing Namsilat over his head. Having played this game a few times however, Namsilat tumbled over the mounts head and landed on his feet. The Talon drawn, his eyes fell on Clifford towering over five miniature people frozen in terror standing next to the huge body of the Hydra, they had somehow managed to pull most of the way out of the swamp.

"Halflings, I should have known. I should let him eat you just for trying to steal my horse." Namsilat looked at the small men trembling before Clifford.

"We stopped him from running away good sir. We thought you would be grateful," one of the small men spoke.

"You thought I would be killed and you would make off with my goods more likely. I have heard of your kind. It is said you have offered yourselves up as abandoned children to caravans passing through these murky lands, then to repay their kindness for taking you in....you rob them in their SLEEP!" As he raised his voice, Clifford growled and leaned towards the shaking man.

"No sir. I beg you, we meant no harm...we are a weak people, farmers...we saw you fighting the creature and feared when you had defeated it, you would take poorly to our lack of assistance. We thought better to stay your horse for you. I swear." The huge wolf lowered his head between his shoulders and slowly stepped towards the small band.

"He doesn't like being snuck up on and neither do I." Namsilat was now taunting the small men; he knew very little of Halflings and what he did know didn't endear them to him as a race.

"Please kind sir, do not let your beast eat us... we only wanted the creatures heart. We will leave you to your prize, if you will but call him off." One of the men now stood as if accepting his fate at the gallows.

"So you were going to steal from me, and then what? Ambush us when we returned? I have heard of travelers lost in these swamps. Rumor has it your 'people' have intentionally led them to their fate so you could rob them. How say you now, thief?" Clifford still stood guard, his hot breath beating down on them.

"Clifford back." With that the beast stepped back, eyes locked on the group, body postured to pounce if given the word or reason.

"It...it was for our families sir, we are simple farmers not thieves. The last two seasons have left us barren. I beg of you; if you must punish any of us, let it be me. I am the leader of the hunting party and as such I shall take full responsibility for attempting to take your…"

"Steal!" Namsilat shouted.

"…to steal your bounty." As he spoke the small band parted allowing him to step forward. Namsilat got his first real look at the Halflings. From their dress he could tell they were most probably farmers just as the little man had said. None carried so much as a bow, sword or even a sling, only simple daggers. He assumed the one standing before him to be the eldest and the leader as he had said. Matted, shoulder-length grey hair hung down over his face, hiding most of it. But the Halfling's eyes were impossible to hide. Deep ocean blue, wide and bright as the sun, innocence was betrayed only by his obvious age. Namsilat had only met one other Halfling that encounter had been uneasy at first and Ish would be hard pressed not to turn you into something if you ever called him 'Halfling'. The Gnomes believed they were an entirely different race. Namsilat figured if they hailed from society they were 'Gnomes' and if they lived in the wilderness they were 'Halflings', no real matter to him.

"But I swear on my word sir, we were not intent on harming you or stealing your fine steed."

"Your honor has not been established here sir. If you, as you say, are farmers, then you must surely know these lands well." Namsilat figured he would get the information he needed before he let them off the hook. "Tell me then, I wish to reach the great mountain known as Mount Hood. Which direction is out of this swamp you profess to call home?" He waved his sword around them, pointing in various directions. The small man lowered his head and stepped slowly forward. Clifford stepped between them, stopping the man's approach.

"He thinks you are close enough to speak." Namsilat warned.

"I do not know the way I fear, I can only offer myself as a guide. I know the routes around the dangers and where the Orc lands lay. Eventually I will find you a path if you will allow my sons to return to their families." The man knelt.

"Rise creature, I am no noble that you should bow. I see your words are true, enough of this, Clifford." With that the huge beast closed on the man, his eyes locked, his breath still panting as his mouth opened widely and his tongue flicked out covering the man in slobber as he nuzzled up to him.

"I am Namsilat, a little lost at the moment and thought for sure we were Hydra bait. So tell me, to whom do I speak?" Namsilat sheathed the Talon and held out his hand. The trembling man stood and smiled as he reached out for the huge hand.

"I am Altaron Needle Fang; these are my sons Lowen, Jastfar, Bar'rey and Toe." The men bowed as they were announced. Well met to you, Namsilat. I, we, are truly sorry we have caused you to tarry. My sons will help you retrieve the beast if you wish and then you and I can set out to find this great Hood Mountain of yours". His voice indicated his uncertainty.

"My prize? If your people are so desperate as to eat the flesh of one of those beasts, by all means you are welcome to it." Namsilat looked at the men in curious disgust.

Namsilat turned to Lester. "As for your offer to 'guide' me; I have heard the blind leading the blind is not a good journey. I shall leave you to your lands." He threw his leg up over Lester. Clifford had now drenched the others in Dire wolf drool and wrestled with them as Namsilat saddled up. "Cliff."

"It's the heart good sir. I feel I must tell you the true value of your treasure, lest you short yourself ignorantly. The heart of the Hydra contains extreme magical properties and is highly sought by mages for that reason. We will retrieve it for you and you will make a fortune. I could never ask, after all that we have troubled you, that you give such a great reward. It is yours, won fair and square in the defeat of the beast. You have done us a great service in slaying it, now we can hunt these lands again without fear. That will be of great help to my people." He waved his hands and Toe, the youngest of the lot, raced back up the side of the huge dead creature and shouted with great excitement.

"I'll get it." He thrust his tiny dagger under the scale of the beast and began working to cut it open. Once he had hacked his way through the thick hide, the small being shoved his arm deep into the cavity of the Hydra and began feeling around. "I got it, I got it." Namsilat did not share the excitement of being covered in the disgusting goo, and when he saw the 'prize' it did not make him any more thrilled. The man hoped off the beast and ran to his father holding a blob of slimy black nothingness.

"You're going to trade that for great riches?" Namsilat asked as the older man took the blob.

"Oh by the Goddess that I were, no, my friend, you shall be rich beyond your dreams. These have been traded for lands, in some stories our people share, for maidens and gold." His eyes sparkled even brighter than before.

"To the blind or infirm I fear sir. I couldn't even burden Lester to carry such a disgusting mass; Clifford, however, I am sure would make a quick snack of it. No, I am still on…you keep it." With that he patted for Clifford to join him as he turned Lester away.

"Sir, please wait. I shall reveal its true nature." Namsilat looked back over his shoulder as Altaron placed the blob on the earth. A sunbeam, as if directed by some unseen source, locked on the mass and within seconds it dried and became a hardened block the size of Namsilat's fist. Altaron fetched it up and held it before him.

"No, still nothing." Namsilat teased. Ignoring him, Altaron took out his tiny dagger and held it by its blade. The others gathered round like dwarves awaiting the cask to be open. Namsilat watched, half in curiosity, as the man smashed his dagger handle down hard on the stone. There was a loud cracking sound that Namsilat took to be the dagger handle breaking. Then the harden shell split and fell away leaving the biggest Black Diamond he had ever seen. The gasp from the group informed him *this* was the prize.

"Nice." He slipped off Lester and returned to the group. Altaron offered him the gem. "I am many things sir, but I do not give a gift and then in seeing its 'value', take it back. I have given your people this token. If it will serve to feed them, let it be so."

The entire group of small beings surrounded him, hugging his legs, almost knocking him down. Tears swelled up in Altaron's eyes and he swallowed hard.

"You sir, are noble. I do not know of this mountain you seek, but there is one in our village that has traveled much. He may know of your desire. And my people will want to thank the one who so selflessly has given what is the most powerful of gifts. You must come with us and let our people thank you. We have little, but there shall be a feast." Altaron again bowed, his sons now joining him.

"Please, you owe me nothing. If this friend knows the passage I seek, I shall be in your debt. I will accept your gracious offer, but rise. We are all free men here." Namsilat took up Lester's reins and followed the band for most of the rest of the day to their tiny village.

* * * * *

In the Temple of Atheria, in the SilverLeaf Village, Airapal prayed to the Goddess. In a vision a dark figure appeared and approached her. "Tar a Mus, is that you?" she whispered. The figure stopped at the base of the great stairs. A cold breeze drifted in, a foul smell assaulted her nose drowning out the sweet incense of the temple censures. "Tar a Mus?"

The dark figure looked up, its eyes empty and void of any life. "I am so cold. Where am I?" It moaned with the voice of the damned.

"Tar a Mus, you are home. It is I, Airapal, your betrothed.

"Airapal, Airapal! You must help me…I, I can't resist much longer. Please Airapal you must…" As it spoke the figure began to shimmer and fade. Just as their eyes met the figure lunged at the High Priestess of Atheria. She threw up her hands to block the attack.

"Priestess, Airapal! Airapal, can you hear me? Are you alright?" The voice of her assistant, Dana, called to her from the void. As she came out of her trance she was soaked and shaking. Her heart pounded in her chest, she gasped for air. "AIRAPAL!" Dana rushed to her side.

"Where is he?" Airapal began looking around desperately.

"Who, Priestess?"

"Tar a Mus, he…he was just here." She gazed towards the statue of the Goddess.

"You were in a trance, my lady. It must have been his spirit, but I thought he was your life mate." The younger woman looked confused.

"He was…why do you say it like that?" Airapal looked up.

"You were fighting so fiercely when I entered." The young woman knelt beside her.

"Something is terribly wrong. Dana, summons the Priests, all of them. Evil has set against the living and we must find its source." Airapal stood and ordered her young assistant out.

As Dana raced away to summons the priests, Airapal turned to the statue… "I am coming my Love *this* I promise." She grasped her holy symbol and bowed to the Goddess.

CHAPTER 3

The Halfling people were a little reserved around the big man who entered their village. Most of their encounters with humans, of any blood, had been unpleasant at best. Many of the younger Halflings had never even seen a human, and Dire wolves were things of nightmares and scary stories to keep children in at night. When the Sage declared Namsilat an honorary Halfling, the small beings accepted him fully.

"You have saved our village by your unselfish act of great generosity, and we shall be forever in your debt. You and your beast will always find food and shelter amongst our people. We shall recite your wondrous doings through all the Halfling realms and you shall be known by our people as Namsilat the Great." With F'lon's pronouncement the village cheered.

After the proclamation, Namsilat and F'lon spent the next few hours discussing the adventuring life. F'lon had spent many of his younger years traveling the Columbia Gorge; he spoke of the early encounters with the great fire demons, the Dragons, and a time when the Dragon war raged heavy in the lands. He had seen the first Kingdom grow into the great Coeur D'Alene of today. He had witnessed the rise of the Dark one and had seen his defeat at the hand of King Darrin's riders. F'lon was a true adventurer. It was only when his people needed his guidance that he retired from that life and took up as their Sage. He helped Namsilat plan out the safest, if not, the quickest route over the valley to the Hood River which would lead him in time to the Gorge.

"You will want to stay clear of Re'dMond; the Orcs have been sending scouts out this way, spying on the good Elf peoples in SilverLeaf. My experience tells me that when they are scouting, they are up to no good. A lone traveler would make easy prey for a band of scouts. They have been a little testy ever since the young King cut them off from their cousins over in MedFord."

"I would swing out over the Willamette and cut through the Wilderness along the Hood's base. Beware however, rumor is that the Fire Demon residing there has risen and she is a fierce beast. Your pet would be poor defense and your mount a simple snack for her." F'lon offered his knowledge.

"What of the WarmSpring people? What do you know of them?" Namsilat asked, thinking the low route, though filled with Orcs, might save him a few days travel.

"Fierce warriors, but sensible people, they do not to my knowledge attack weary travelers. Most encounters between our peoples have been peaceful." As F'lon spoke a young fair-haired child gathered her courage and climbed right up into Namsilat's lap.

"Curlina! You come here right this instant." Her small Halfling mother scolded, standing off to the side of the men not wanting to interrupt. "Can't you see F'lon and the human are speaking?" The small child simply held up her rag doll for Namsilat's approval.

"Her name is Tawnie. My mommy made her for me. You can hold her if you want to." A giant smile ran across her tiny face as the big man stretched out his arms, encircling her and taking Tawnie in his giant hands.

"Curlina!" her mother shouted, stepping in to retrieve the arrant child.

"Oh, it's alright. I believe we are finished here." Namsilat assured the frantic woman.

"Tawnie has never met a giant before." The young girl's eyes studied the big man as he admired the rag doll. The three began to laugh.

"Well, I have never been a giant before." Namsilat mused. "So what is your name little one?"

"My name is Becca, but folks around here call me 'Curlina', on account I like to curl up in laps." She informed him.

"You do? I would have never guessed."

As Namsilat was making friends with Becca and Tawnie, Clifford had been busy making friends of his own, giving rides, despite his objection to all the small children in the village. They rode him until he tired of it and simply walked over and plopped himself down at Namsilat's feet.

"Had enough?" Namsilat teased as the last of the riders gave up.

"You have a long journey ahead of you my friend. I shall let you get some rest. I know an early start is a good start. Again I thank you on behave of my entire village Namsilat. We hope you and Clifford will visit often." F'lon stood and bid Namsilat a good night.

"That we shall do, you and your people have made a special place in my heart F'lon. I swear we shall visit here whenever the Fates bring us this way. Nothing personal, but I do hope it is not too often." He smiled. "May the Gods bless your harvest and may your life be filled with bounty. We shall depart at first light. Namsilat stood as F'lon walked away.

CHAPTER 4

Namsilat tossed and turned most of the night, his long frame barely fitting between the walls of the small hut. The morning sun found him less than excited to climb, once more, into the saddle and head out into the swamp. He wanted to reach the Kingdom before first snow, and he still had several stops to make. The path they had laid out would take him a few hundred miles off his original route. Back-tracking to SilverLeaf would only lead to another winter spent wishing he was out adventuring. The almost two years had been wonderful and departing was a task, especially with Airapal offering him a permanent home with her people. It sounded a lot like settling down to him.

Morning birds sang their songs and flitted around in the tree branches, catching insects that had raided the tiny village in the night. The Halfling people had already begun their daily chores as Namsilat made his way to Lester. It was not a surprise to him that Lester had already saddled and a sack of food hung from the saddle, a large dried bone hung attached to it. It was the gift tied to the saddle horn that almost brought a tear to the traveler. Tawnie, the little rag doll of Becca, sat ready to ride. Stuffing back the emotions he tried to keep at bay, he turned to Lester.

"What? One night in town and you will let just anybody saddle you?" Taking the small doll off the saddle, he tucked it securely inside the fine leather vest Airapal had given him. He rode quietly out of the village headed east; the first leg of the journey would take him along the bottom of the swampy Tigard drain and into the foot hills of the WarmSpring people. With any luck, by nightfall he would be deep within the plush evergreens that make up much of Mount Hood's forest.

The trio traveled smoothly most of the morning. As the mid-day sun hung high in the sky they took their first break. Clifford had made his hunger clear and Namsilat knew trying to get him to travel on anything less than a full stomach would be a fight. He had made it difficult for Lester to keep moving, dancing around the horse darting between his legs wagging his tail and generally agitating the animal.

"Alright already! It's too hot to argue. Go find us some shade and we will eat." Namsilat had no more gotten the words out when the huge canine rushed off into the brush. Within seconds his low, groaning howl announced he had found a suitable resting place.

To Namsilat's relief this time there was actually room for both, as well as shade for Lester. The last time he tried that, Clifford had found the closest bush and plopped down under it. He knew there was no point in arguing so he and Lester had stood for that meal. Swinging off Lester he tossed the huge bone to Clifford and was untying the grain sack when he noticed the tall, dark plume of smoke rising in the air behind them, in the direction of the Halfling village.

"Whoa, that can't be good. You're gonna have to wait for mid-day meal ole' buddy." He tied the sack back onto the saddle. "Come on Clifford. I fear our friends may be in trouble."

He threw himself into the saddle and slapped the strap across Lester's butt. They took off west; rushing across the land they had just spent the morning covering. Though they hadn't been traveling fast, at this pace it would still take them the better part of the day to return. Clifford had taken the lead and rushed across the humid terrain. The heat had little effect on him but Lester was feeling it as they reached the outskirts of the small village.

Flames still roared from several of the tiny huts. Bodies lay strewn everywhere. Namsilat pulled Lester to a halt just on the edge of the village; he jumped off and came up sword in hand as he scanned the village for signs of life…any life. Clifford took his place at Namsilat's side as they began the search. Even the farm animals had been slain, but by who and why?

"What the Hells?" Namsilat continued to scan for survivors as he and Clifford made their way through the carnage. Clifford swung out taking the right side of the village as Namsilat walked cautiously up the left. He looked at several of the bodies as he passed, arrows protruded from them, some in front, but many from the back. Closer examination revealed them to be Orc arrows but why would they attack a village of farmers and take nothing? He made his way to F'lon's hut at the center of the village. The Sage lay face down on his porch, a pool of blood covering the ground beneath him, his hand out-stretched as if offering something.

"The Heart?" the word left Namsilat's lips with a bad taste.

Something didn't add up and Namsilat knew it. Orcs are many things, but even they are not given to kill an entire village to steal a single item. No, an Orc raiding party would have simply come in, stole the thing, taken the animals and left the villagers to the fates. As he walked back through the street he noticed several of the bodies had been cut almost in half by a strong sword blow. Whoever had done this had shown no mercy. In the growing darkness he knew he would not find good tracks. His best bet would be to wait until morning, so he set to the task of burying the dead.

Clifford approached slowly out of the darkness, the lifeless body of little Becca dangling from his jaws. He gently laid the young girl at Namsilat's feet. "There is no excuse for this sort of senseless killing." Taking her body in his hands he held her up to the Goddess. "They shall pay for this, I swear it." He spent most of the night gathering and burying the dead. As he laid little 'Curlina's' body in her grave, he placed Tawnie in with her to keep her company in the dark earth. He placed several boards and stones over the grave, it would not keep the carrion out for long, but it was the least he could do.

CHAPTER 5

Morning birds sang as the sun brought first light. The dead buried, he now would search the entire village for any tracks he could follow. There were several riders and at least five footmen. They would not travel fast, he sent Clifford out to get their trail. He and Lester would ride hard and Clifford would wait for them once he located the group. At least that is what Namsilat had told him to do. He gathered up several of the arrows, a fitting justice he figured, to be killed by their own weapons.

The trail lead northeast, Namsilat was a little surprised he had not seen them on his return. He had been following the trail for an hour when Clifford howled. The howl had not come from in front of him as he had expected, but off to the West, almost cutting back behind him. He turned Lester and drove hard for the next two hours before finding the huge, red wolf sitting on a ledge overlooking the Sandy River. He quickly got his bearings; they were heading back towards the southlands and freedom. They would have to cut around the SilverLeaf valley. If the Elves found them first, they would be dead before he could extract his revenge. He hoped the river would slow them, if not stop them all together. He gathered Clifford and started down the dusty cliff bank to the shoreline. He got off and looked for signs of their heading.

"Huh now, what's this? It looks like several of the mounts turned north towards Sandy but the footmen have continued south, probably running home."

Namsilat lead Lester across the rapid stream. The river at this time of the year can be shallow in places, but the Sandy is never to be underestimated. It is swift and unforgiving if you do. Coming out on the west bank he searched for the rider's tracks. Four had continued up the west bank towards the north which would lead them straight into the town of Sandy, and Orcs would not be welcomed there. He didn't figure that the overwhelming success in the Halflings village would have filled them with such confidence they would take on the whole of Sandy. This was getting more confusing by the minute. There were at least ten more mounts that had turned along the river, probably as support for the foot travelers. He wanted to know why Orcs were going towards a human settlement. So he mounted Lester and pushed him up the bank towards Sandy.

They traveled along the ledge above the river; staying just inside the tree line to allow him to watch the river, should they be setting up a diversion and planning to backtrack through the river itself. The Sandy flowed north from Mount Hood, eventually dumping into the Great Columbia. Just twenty miles from its mouth sat the human town of Sandy, more of a stockade than an actual town. It had been established as a stronghold when the Orc wars had ended, giving the King's men a safe haven to guard the border. It also was the location of one of the richest iron mines along the southern lands of Coeur D'Alene. Though well fortified, the Orcs had constantly made raids on it, but never overrunning it. He had never heard of a band as small as four ever even trying.

He thought to cut around them and warn the gate men, but he figured if they turned and ran he would be waiting with open arms and loaded bow. From high on the river's edge, if they did decide to cut back, he would have an excellent firing position and offer them no hiding place from his arrows. They would have to cross at the sand bar, if they were in fact going to Sandy. He waited until nightfall and then pushed Lester out towards the west and cut around the slower moving band. With luck he would catch them as they crossed and the river could wash their dead bodies out to the Columbia for fish bait. He had Clifford continue on; he would let out a howl if they turned back now. As the sun rose he sat on Lester and waited…as the hours passed, nothing. Lester was getting edgy as Clifford came meandering out of the brush on the edge of the sand bar.

"What? Did they turn back?" No, Clifford would have sensed them. They must have passed through already. He would inquire with the gate men. It was five miles from the sand bar to the town gates. Perhaps they had already met their fate there. As he reached the small wooden bridge leading into town he looked for signs of a fight, but nothing. A voice caught his attention as he crossed the bridge.

"Welcome wanderer, welcome to Sandy." A well-dressed guard waved down at him from the gate shack.

"Good day kind sir. Have you seen any Orcs this day or perhaps last eve?" Namsilat sat in his saddle and looked around him, back towards the river bank.

"Orcs? Why no sir. We have not seen those creatures in months. Were you attacked?" the man asked.

"No, I thought I was following a band of them however. I found signs in a small village they ransacked out in the Swamps of Tigard, and they were headed this way as early as last night."

"Only had four riders come this way last night, a group of mercenaries. They are held up over at the Goats Head. Been there drinking and bragging all night." The man offered suddenly his head went up and he grabbed his long bow and notched an arrow. Namsilat thought perhaps the Orcs had slipped up on him and he drew his blade, turning Lester quickly to meet the attack.

"Quickly sir, into the gate before the beast strikes" the man's voice called down. Namsilat spotted Clifford walking slowly towards him.

"Fire not sir, that is my companion and he means no ill. He is simply returning to my side." Namsilat had spent the last two years away from humans, Clifford had been so openly welcomed by the Elves he forgot what the sight of a Dire wolf does to most. "Clifford stop I'll come to you."

With that Namsilat rode out and retrieved the huge animal, leading him past the quaking guards as they entered the township. "You say these fellows are bragging, huh. What do they have to be so proud of?" Namsilat asked as he pulled up inside the gate.

"Seems they killed themselves a Hydra, even have the black heart diamond to prove it." One of the guards shouted out. Rage flushed through Namsilat. Could he have been duped? "It's quite the item if you've never seen one, probably won't get a chance to see another one in your lifetime." The man continued.

"Where did you say these men were?" Namsilat's eyes followed his arm as the sentry pointed across the busy street towards an old inn, above the door a rotting sign barely hung on.

Goats Head Inn

Namsilat tied Lester off; pointing at the ground under him he turned to Clifford. The huge animal curled up under the horse as Namsilat stepped onto the wooden plank walkway that ran the length of the building. "You stay here and I'll feed you when I come out. And no begging, neither one of you."

Stepping inside Namsilat stood for several seconds allowing his eyes to adjust to the darkened interior. The smell of fresh food was overrun by the stench of stale ale and spilt wine. Loud bolstering voices boomed from across the room and it didn't take him long to find the men. There were four, dressed in various adventuring gear, sitting at a small table surrounded by several curious, free drinkers. The man straight across the table wore simple hide armor with a thick fur collar. To his right, a slightly smaller man wearing piecemeal chain armor. The man with his back to Namsilat was by far the largest of the four, he figured him to be a good foot taller than himself, donning thick hide armor with an even taller fur collar than the first man. A large maul rested against the table to his left. The last man Namsilat took for a rogue. He wore soft grey leather, a bone handled dagger rested on his right hip.

42

Namsilat figured he had several unexposed weapons tucked inside boots and under the dark silk cloak thrown back over his left shoulder. Sitting dead center of the table was the heart. As he started across the dark room with one thought in his mind, a voice off to the right called to him.

"Good sir, care for a mid-day meal or perhaps just a simple ale to wash down the trail dirt?" A stout little dwarf stood in the doorway leading into the kitchen.

Namsilat paused, took a deep breath and realized just walking in and attacking these four fellows would not look good. Though confident in his ability to handle the likes of them, the city guard would be a task.

"They both sound delightful actually. I'll try the pork." He wandered over to the bar just across from the table where the four braggarts sat.

"House special, pork and a tankard of ale...that's two copper." The dwarf drew up a tin cup of thick ale and plated up a slab of fresh roasted pork for the new customer. "Comes with bread

43

as well." He placed the plate down on the bar in front of Namsilat. Namsilat produced two coins and tossed them on the bar. With a nod the dwarf picked up the coins and exited into the kitchen.

"Sing, Bard." the man sitting against the back wall shouted out. Tilting his cup up, Namsilat scanned the table again. The rogue would be the wild card; the man against the wall would be straight forward, too full of himself to think a single opponent a real threat. The Chainmail fool was too self-concerned to throw himself in, he would hesitate. The big man's weapon was too slow to concern Namsilat, in this close of a space he could cut the man three times before he could even get the weapon up. The rogue was already aware of Namsilat's attention; they gave each other a nod as their eyes met. He would be on guard.

"Sing, I said, or repay my friend's generous offering." The big man tossed a full mug of ale at the small minstrel.

"How's your meal?" The dwarf had returned. For the first time Namsilat took a sniff of the hot fresh meal, the first meal he would not have to share with Clifford in a very long time.

"Smells wondrous. Tell me, good sir, what is their occasion for such drunkenness at this early hour?" Namsilat let his voice carry across the room.

"Oh, they have been drunk since last evening actually. It seems they ran into a Hydra out in the Swamp and were fortunate enough to get the best of the creature. Been bragging all night. Their coin is good, so I haven't run them out...yet!" The dwarf raised his voice looking over at the group with a warning.

Namsilat had just taken a sip of his ale and made a scene spitting it back out. "Really, a real feat for any I must say." Namsilat did his best to temper his words.

"Yeah, they said it damn near killed the big guy there, says his name is Adarrass." The dwarf offered.

"Hmmm, does he now? Sounds kind of like 'hand me my ass, doesn't it?" Namsilat felt the anger building. He watched out of the corner of his eye as the rogue slipped his chair back and away from the table. The trembling Bard froze in his tune. The group fell silent. Tension grew, filling the room. The big man let out a deep laugh, the Bard snickered and the group fell into laughter and returned to taunting the Bard. The dwarf leaned in close to Namsilat's ear and whispered his warning.

"Sir, I would caution you, they have had more than five men's share of ale this morn alone. I would just finish up your meal and be on your way. I am quite sure the big man heard you. I have seen many of their kind; they are not given to overlook insult…even if offered in jest." The dwarf warned.

"I have seen their kind as well." Namsilat responded. " I thank you for your concern, but I wish to enjoy my meal and I doubt Load of Ass there is going to do much more than taunt an unarmed man or perhaps kill innocent children." Namsilat spoke clearly; looking at the rogue he shook his head in discouragement as the man reached for his dagger. The young Bard did his best to sing over the taunt. Adarrass raised his tankard and slammed it on the table.

"Bar keep! More ale I'll buy for everyone…even the Half." He held his mug out, using it to point at Namsilat. Namsilat held up his mug and offered his own salute.

"To your great courage and generosity Pat my Ass." The entire bar fell silent; several patrons rushed out the exit.

"Sir, please, I ask that you finish and leave. I have no desire to have your blood spilled in my establishment...now please." The dwarf placed his hand on Namsilat's.

The man sitting with his back against the wall picked up the bag and the gem off the table.

"Do you know what this is, Half-blood?" He held it towards Namsilat.

"Let me guess. It is the black heart of a Hydra, you four losers supposedly took from the fierce beast, after it damn near killed Fat Ass there. Close?" Namsilat smirked, using his mug to point at Adarrass.

"That it is, the beast so awful, you sir, would have soiled your breeches. If it were not for Adarrass's swift and fearless actions, it would have killed the lot of us. So if you are to continue this disrespectful slander, and I speak for us all... "he waved his hands around the circle..." we shall defend his honor."

"Honor? Why the word itself must be as strange to your mouth, as its meaning is to a cowardly lot such as you. If you faced this dreaded creature, tell me this, brave 'smells of Ass', how many heads did it have?" Namsilat sat facing the men now, his eye watching the rogue's every move as he taunted the group.

"Five, four, it was three"…each man offering up a different answer in turn stumbling over each other.

"You are too humble, for I believe the creature you took that heart from had at least thirty heads. You are a bunch of lying cowards and I intend to see you face justice for your act." Namsilat felt the Dwarf's hand grasp his arm.

"You, sir, will leave my inn NOW!" He drew Namsilat up by the arm and thrust him towards the door. "Do not be so foolish to presume me a coward. I assure you I will use this." the man's eyes glanced down; Namsilat looked and saw that he held a small crossbow pointed at his stomach. "Now, set down the tankard slowly and depart. I will hold them but a moment. The guards are across the square, I suggest you run." With that he stepped aside and pointed to the door. Namsilat gently lowered the tankard and stepped away from the bar, keeping his eyes on the men as he walked out.

The men sat for just a moment then stood and walked to the door. The dwarf walked back into the kitchen, in his eyes the fool had asked for it.

Adarrass was the first to the door, followed closely by the rogue. As he threw the door open and stepped out, he quickly stumbled back, forcing the rogue to catch him. Blood squirted from his open mouth, the shaft of an Orc arrow protruding from his throat. A scream came from somewhere to the left. The men looked up. Namsilat stood just outside the door, bow drawn and pointing straight at them.

The chainmail man stepped out to the right mumbling…"Rob us if you must, but by the Gods, sir, who murders an unarmed man in broad daylight? He tossed the bag holding the stone at Namsilat's feet and the three men fell to their knees as if begging for mercy. The rogue looked up into Namsilat's eyes and a smile ran across his face. Clifford growled and Namsilat looked to his side. The city guards had responded to the scream and now closed in on him.

"Lower your weapon sir, or we will be forced to fire on you." The guards raised their crossbows and stood their ground. Clifford started to rise up, Namsilat held out his hand, stopping him and dropping his bow in the same motion. No need to get them all killed here. "Theft is taken very seriously here sir, and a murder committed in the act of doing so is a hanging offense. What have you to say for yourself?" The guard signaled for the three men to move away from the supposed bandit. Another guard walked up and grabbed his bow off the ground, as he reached for Namsilat's sword the adventurer warned him.

"I would not touch that if I were you sir. The weapon is much attached to me and well, if one should touch it without my consent it tends to be painful at best." With his warning the guard froze his fingers only inches away from the hilt.

"Remove your sword sir, and toss it away. If the item is in fact hexed, we will have our mage retrieve it." The lead guard ordered and Namsilat did as he was told. He knew the Talon was only a thought away at any moment, but no need to tell them that little fact.

"Am I to be arrested and hanged without giving my side to this mishap? I would think in the King's land justice would be accepted and better treated. These men are the thieves. I have been tracking them for two days. They slaughtered an entire village of Halflings for the stone in that pouch, not a Hydra as they profess. As for murder, I shall plead that these men had followed me out, intent on my being harmed." Namsilat had a feeling his words were falling on deaf ears and to make matters worse, if they could be, the rogue pointed out the obvious.

"Would you take the word of a Half-blood over that of three loyal subjects of the King, sir?" The man looked around, stirring up the crowd. The rogue then rolled Adarrass's body over, exposing the Orcish arrow sticking out of his throat. There was a gasp from the now rather large crowd. "Look, he even uses Orc arrows. What sort of gentleman uses such a disgusting creature's weapon?" with that he all but sealed Namsilat's fate. He would have to allow himself to be arrested and just catch up with these cowards once he escaped.

Namsilat simply turned and began walking towards the guard house; he knew was located at the gate. "I shall await you at the jail, good sirs." As several of the guards rushed up to him, he turned and smiled at the rogue.

"He has murdered our friend and tried to rob us in mid-day. Surely you will not allow this to go unpunished. We demand he be hung!" The rogue shouted as they lead Namsilat away.

"The captain of the guard is gone and will not return until morning. I cannot hang a man without his consent. I assure the Captain is a fair man; and justice will be served." With that he picked up the bag holding the gem and turned to go after his men.

"Why are you taking our goods? We have done nothing." The rogue objected.

"That too shall be the Captains call. As I have said, he is a fair man. There is a cost however for execution, and someone will be taxed to pay it." The guard smiled as he slipped the pouch into his

belt.

CHAPTER 6

The day passed slower than Namsilat thought a day could. Night finally fell and Namsilat settled in for a long night of self-examination. He knew that if he had been a little more discrete he could have saved himself a lot of trouble. But the sight of little Becca laying there in the cold ground as he buried her kept flashing in his mind, along with the audacity of those braggarts to flaunt the worthless stone that had cost an entire village of good people their life. He regretted ever killing the damn thing, even entering the Swamp was a fool's error. He would just sit out the night and answer to the captain; at least he had extracted revenge on one of the spineless vermin. Outside the cage he could hear Clifford begin to snore, at least one of them could sleep.

Namsilat woke to the sound of clanging chain being removed from the cell door. His eyes squinted against the early morning sunlight as the large figure of a man crossed in front of the doorway as it opened. Namsilat raised his arm to block out some of the sun and felt the heavy weight as something large pounced on him and the rough wet texture of a tongue. It felt as if it were peeling off skin with each swipe it made against his bare skin.

"Hey, get off me you big oaf!" he shouted in protest as Clifford lavished him with his to kisses.

"Pup's awful glad to see you?" the large man grunted as he waved for the pair to come out of the cage.

"Am I to hurry to my fate?" Namsilat grumbled as he swaggered towards the opening. He was met by another voice, as he stood straight.

"It would seem that your fate is to wait for you this day, sir. It would also appear that I owe you an apology."

Namsilat looked to the voice. It was the guard that had placed him in the cell. "Oh, is that so?"

"Yes. It seems that your accusers were indeed the thieves you said they were. Sometime in the night they roughed up one of my guards and made their escape. So other than the price of burying the body and last evening's meal…"

"I received no meal!" Namsilat started to protest.

"No. But your beast there ate. Several chickens and we are still looking for a small dog that came up missing." The captain offered.

Namsilat gave Clifford a very stern look. "How much do I owe?"

"Your debt was paid by your friend already."

Again the fighter glanced at the huge red pup.

"Not him, sir, your friend over at the Goats Head. He arrived this morning and was greeted by your animal there. From the way the beast has responded to everyone else in town, I had no problem believing he knew you when he asked for your whereabouts. I informed him that you were awaiting trial. That was before I learned the criminals had absconded. He said he would be waiting to buy you a good meal and hearty drink.

Namsilat looked down at Clifford. Who could have shown up here that knew him? Had the brothers wandered in from their trip up the Mount Hood? No there would be four of them. He wondered

who it could be all the way to the inn. As he stepped into the

darkened bar, his elfin vision perked up, scanning the area for

bodies. There were only three tables that had customers. Two

humans sat and laughed jokingly about the small miserable mutt that

had gone missing from old lady Haygus's place and all the upset

chicken farmers that had gone out of business last night. Namsilat

was not sure he wanted to stay around here too long. The other table

was taken by what looked like a small child devouring a rather large

meal. He looked to the third table then back to the child.

"ISH! Ish is that you?" Namsilat made a rush to the table and

Clifford followed close behind. The small man stood as they

approached and hopped up on the table to give him an embrace.

"Namsilat, I thought I had seen the last of you. What brings

you to this less than reputable little hole?" The mage asked as he

looked around.

"Hey, I told the guards that beast could not be in here" the

barkeep shouted as he advanced on the group.

GGGRRRRrrrr!!! Clifford turned and met the Dwarf halfway to the table.

"He is my companion and not a beast. Lucky for you, I hear, he has already eaten this day." The pair chuckled as the man turned and made his way back behind the bar. "I had a little run in with some strange fellows and their trail led me here. I was working on setting the problem straight when I was accused of theft and tossed in the cellar. I figured I was gonna have to fight my way out of here but I guess they made off in the night." Namsilat shuffled through his pack and brought out his coin purse. "I hear I owe you for some chickens and perhaps a dog?" he looked down at Clifford now lying at his feet.

"You owe me nothing my friend. I am just glad I was able to do you a good turn. So where does your road lead from here?" Ish returned to his meal.

"I had no real destination in mind. That was of course before this band crossed my path. I was thinking of heading towards the Kingdom, I hear there is to be a huge celebration for the young

Prince turning of age. Figured I might find word on some new adventure or even hook up with a group setting out for fame and fortune. Perhaps find some word on these men, and you? Where are the fates taking the great 'Ishvanvarminstine' this fine day?

"Well, I had heard of the Prince's party, but I also know that the Festival of Spring is starting over in PortsLand at this same time. I thought perhaps I would start there and…" with a wave of his hand, he pronounced…"then pop up to the celebration."

"I might wander through PortsLand as well, but I have never been to the Kingdom, and I have sort of been longing to see why all those people crowd into one place."

"We could venture a bit together if you were interested, and I could take you along when I pop over."

"I kind of want to find these fellows again. I still feel a little indebted to them and they still have something I intend to retrieve?"

"Did they rob you, my friend?"

"Not in so many words."

Ish lowered his voice and leaned in closer to Namsilat. "Do you intend to rob them?"

"NO! I have not taken up that sort of life as of yet, Ish."

"Didn't think so. Just thought that maybe I should ask. Times have been hard on many. I know a man...

"Ish."

"You're right. Enough said. Let us eat and speak of better things and better times." He lifted his glass in a toast. As they clanked glasses, the bright metal medallion swung from under Namsilat's blouse. The coin of gold and silver, its tiny sword and holly leaf on the blue sapphire backing caught Ish's eye. He reached out and took it in his hand, flipping it over several times, and then looking up into the fighter's eyes.

"How do you come by this coin?" The little man's body posture took a twist Namsilat had learned to be a warning. He pulled the coin from his hand and leaned away from his friend.

"It is, or was, my father's. It is the only thing he left my mother before he went off and got himself killed fighting in the Southern War. Why, do know it?" Namsilat felt the old feeling of hope grow. Did his friend know his father; could he tell him more about the man he never really got to know? He worked hard not to let his face show it.

"I know of him, I never had occasion to meet the man. But his sacrifice..."

"I know of his sacrifice." Namsilat's voice turned cold.

"You seem unpleased. Do you really know of the deeds your father and..."

"Yes, I know it. It was spoon fed to me as a child by a broken-hearted woman that could not let allow herself to feel the bitterness of being abandoned with a child." Namsilat could not hold back the trembling in his body.

"Do you distain him so much?" Ish asked as he sat back.

"I knew him not. He stole my mother's heart and then took it with him to be buried on some shitty little piece of dirt, which was not even his to defend. And mother and I had to forge our way alone. Do you know how people treat a Half-blood or even worse, the mother of one? To have to move from town to town until you find some farmer who is willing to let you and your 'mistake' live in his old barn. Always keeping to yourself so as not to offend the pure bloods and have to move once more? I think not, my friend!" Namsilat pushed away from the table and began to rise.

"A moment my friend, you have spoken your peace, now let an old fool share a little of his wisdom." Ish placed a firm hand on Namsilat's leg. "You have every right to be hurt, but pain as you have embellished it will eat a man up from the inside out. It is no wonder that you prefer the company of animals." He glanced down at Clifford. "No offense, my friend. You ask if I know how it is to be different. I assure you I do," he said standing, waving his hands up and down his small frame. "You have no corner on that market. As for your mother, it was her heart to give and hers to keep. Hearts are not 'stolen' as you claim. If you had spent a little more time thinking of her and hearing her words, rather than feeling so sorry for yourself, you might have caught a glimpse of the happiness a woman finds in giving her heart to one, and raising the offspring of that union, however unpleasant a task that may prove to be. As for getting himself killed, Ha! I have seen many good men fall in battle, and none of them did it with intent. If you think your father the exception, it shows how little you truly know of him!" Ish's stern eyes glared into Namsilat's.

The two sat in somber silence for several moments. It was Clifford's stirring that finally broke the emptiness. The huge animal raised and leaned against Namsilat. His tail wagging as he looked into his eyes.

"Let me guess, you're hungry?" With that the two started laughing.

"Seems he knows what's important." Ish offered…"Barkeep more food!"

The two ate and drank into the day tossing scraps to Clifford and laughing hysterically as each patron turned and fled the bar as quick as they entered. By mid-day the barkeep had lost all patience and was heading for the table to insist that they leave when Ish rose, swaying, and announced they should be on their way.

"Do you have Lester stabled here? We should fetch him and be gone."

"I believe they put him up, we could…" As Namsilat was beginning to make his suggestion, the little Gnome waved his hand and they were standing outside the stable. The barkeep rushed to the table and was pleasantly surprised to find three gold coins lying there. More than enough to pay for their meals and the lost business he felt they owed him for.

"What if the bar keeps the money?" Namsilat asked as the pair walked into the stable. Lester greeted them with loud neigh.

"I compensated him for his trouble. Now get your steed and let's be off. There are many things we must do, my young friend, before the prince's day."

Namsilat paid the stable bill and saddled Lester, leading him outside where Ish and Clifford waited.

"So where did we decide the fates would have us go?" Namsilat asked as he tossed his leg up over Lester's back. Before his butt had time to settle into the well-worn saddle the dirt beneath him turned to plush green grass. Voices rang in his ears and a cart turned and sped around them. He looked first to Ish, and then began to scold the little mage for the unannounced magic, but his voice fell from him as he gazed ahead, before him stood the grand walls of Coeur D'Alene.

CHAPTER 7

"Clifford will be fine. I'm sure once he has eaten his fill he will let the stable boy out of the shed." Namsilat was telling Ish as they crossed the courtyard. Ish was about to object when the sound of thundering hoof beats bore down on them. Namsilat looked up, seeing a young man on a very large, white horse only a few yards from them, he shouted.

"Look out, you fool!" His hands made an instinctive grab for the little Gnome. Throwing himself out of the path of the wild rider, Ish vanished, leaving Namsilat empty handed as he sailed through the air towards the large fountain in the center of the square. Crashing down inches from the hard stone, Namsilat jumped to his feet just in time to dodge the four riders coming up behind the lead rider. He spotted Tom and started to wave them down, but they were so focused on the first rider they did not notice, to them he was just another angry pedestrian.

"Ish, that looked like Tom and the brothers. Ish?" Namsilat began scouring the street for the smaller man, thinking at last that he

66

must have landed in the fountain. Approaching the fountain he called out to the mage. "Ish!"

"I'm up here. You're not much of an Elf are you?" the small man called down from the top of the white granite statues.

Namsilat glanced up at the high stone figures. Ish stood on the head of a figure of an Elf, chiseled to fine detail; he could almost see the veins in the skin. Over the huge head rested a pair of stone sword handles, Moyie. Next to him stood another Elf, a single sword hanging from his belt, a shield baring the sword and leaf crest Namsilat knew from his childhood, Bonner. His eyes scanned the remaining figures, a Dwarf with a great hammer, Doro. A tall slender human stood to the right and behind the Dwarf, his mighty staff stretching skyward behind them, Hea'fxtrot. A smaller yet more robust human stood front center. King Darrin clad in his magical Armor of the Planes. His helm held proudly in his left arm, his right hand holding the top of his medium shield etched with his family crest, the fruit of the Gods and its leaves in its center.

Namsilat's gaze froze upon the great men he had revered since childhood. These were the King's Riders, with King Darrin in the forefront. These five men had risked their very souls in defense of a Kingdom none of them at the time even called home. They had answered the call against evil and won out. As a child every kid played the game of riders and demons. They always made Namsilat play the demon because he was a Half-blood, but in his heart he was a great warrior, Moyie preferably. Bonner had been the only member of the band to fall. His sacrifice had saved his comrades, but valor was not in Namsilat's nature. Several times the demon had won in their childhood version, for even as a youngster Namsilat was not known to believe things had to go a certain way just because it was written. Life had taught him that at a very young age. Standing here before the figures of these legends, however, he felt the reverence he had forsaken as a lad.

"Awe inspiring, are they not?" Ish's voice reached in and pulled him back to the crowded street. "Do you know who they are?"

"Are you jesting? Every young child in the realms knows who they are, and dreams of being them. They are the King's Riders, saviors of the realms." Namsilat responded, waving his hand over the front of the figures.

"Yes, but do you know who they are?"

"That one is Moyie Spring, Ranger, with his best friend and companion, Bonner Ferrie. Master Doro, the high priest of Thor, and Hea'fxtrot, grand Shaman of the WarmSpring peoples in the southern lands. His majesty, King of Coeur d'Alene and all lands north and south, east and west, to the great ocean is in the lead. Yes, yes I know who they are; they fought against some great evil magic or something."

"*Or SOMETHING.* That would be like saying your dragon quest was a trip in the mountains, my friend."

"Ish, if you please." Namsilat glanced around at the people now staring at them. "I would rather not announce all that to everyone"

"Oh, sorry. I didn't realize that a great dragon slayer such as yourself would be so modest. I care little if these fair folks want to listen in, for I speak not of your heroics, but of those of these great men. If they had not ridden against Condon and the demon Lord ArAGhast you would not be standing where you are, my young Half. This was no 'something'; it was the very demon of the Hells, taker of souls, and tormentor of the damned. His vast army of hell-knights numbered in the thousands, their undead fire-breathing nightmare mounts, chased by a thousand howling hellhounds. Ash and brimstone left in their wake, death and destruction billowing out before them as they descended from the clouds of hell upon the lands. Does this sound like 'or something', to you boy!" The little man had raised his voice so that all around them people had stopped, entranced by the story they all knew, but could never hear enough.

"My apologies my friend, I meant no disrespect to these great men, nor to diminish their heroics in any way, I simply…"

"…have no real idea who these men are, what great sacrifice they made, Bonner Ferrie giving his very life so that the others could escape to continue the fight. No, lad, I know you did not, but I did not bring you here for a history lesson. I just want to make sure that you know what these men really did and who they truly were. They are not legends; they are immortals. Ish leapt down from the edge of the fountain where he had taken up stage to present his point. The crowd began clapping as they disbanded and went back to their lives.

"I get your meaning; I do hold them in high regard as well. I just could not have found the words to express it as you have. Again, I apologize." Namsilat gave a gentle bow to the Gnome.

"I will accept your apology, for I could see the reverence in your eyes as you looked upon their likenesses." Ish began scanning around the crowded streets looking very intently as if searching for some lost or out of place item.

"Are you looking for something, Ish?"

"Someone. Ah you there lad!" A small boy looked over at the mage as he called out. "Yes you. Come here boy." As the child approached, Ish summonsed forth a parchment and quill, scribbling down a quick message he rolled up the parchment and dismissed the pen.

"Yes, sir?" the young man spoke as he approached.

"Do you know the castle well, lad?"

"I know it fair, sir."

"Do you know the great Temple in the Inner Curtain?"

"Yes sir."

"And the grumpy old High Priest is he still there?" Ish knew all too well that he was.

"Master D…"

"Hush yes, that would be he. Do you know him?" Ish pushed.

"Why yes, sir, everyone knows Master Do…"

"Very well, I have a message for him and a gold coin for anyone who might be able to deliver it for me. Do you know someone who might be interested in the task?"

The boy's eyes lit up like an oil fire.

"I could sir! I am the fastest runner in my family, and I'll not tarry either. Straight there I will go. You have my word." With that

Ish produced a gold coin and handed it and the parchment to the lad.

True to his word, he was gone before Ish could even shush him on.

CHAPTER 8

"It is good to be back in the city." Ish announced turning to Namsilat. But Namsilat's attention was drawn off; his eyes were focused hard on something across the street. Ish followed his gaze. In an alleyway thirty yards across from them stood two men, a large muscular human carrying a maul. Next to him stood another man donning piecemeal chain, human, slender in build, sporting a long sword and a short bow. They seemed to be locked in an argument with a merchant, probably over the value of their merchandise. Namsilat seemed very interested and just as Ish was going to ask if he knew the men, Namsilat began moving swiftly in their direction. Ish moved a little to his left and began to follow. From the shift in his stature he could tell that Namsilat's intentions were not to talk. He had made no move for a weapon, but Ish knew he didn't need to.

Crossing in front of several people, Namsilat began to draw comments as he made his way towards the men. About halfway across the street he ran into a fellow, knocking him down. The man hollered out at the fighter, and that got the attention of the two men he was approaching. As soon as their eyes fell upon him, they made a grab at whatever item they had been bantering over and dashed away into the alley, mingling in with crowd. Namsilat rushed towards the alley hoping to catch them before they got too far, but the crowd closed in around them and they vanished as if by magic. He stopped at the merchant's window trying to see over the people. It was then he noticed that they were all starting to give him a wider berth. That's when he felt the hilt of the Talon in his hand; he had not summonsed it unknowingly for almost a year. The vision of little Becca burned in his mind.

"You should probably put that away." Ish's voice came from behind him. Namsilat slid the sword into its scabbard.

"Damn them!" He looked over to the merchant. "Tell me, what were they trying to trade?" The trembling man made an attempt to slide something off the tiny window shelf as Namsilat approached. He looked down and spotted the black leather pouch. His hand snatched it away from the man. "I believe this is mine, do you have some doubt?" The merchant shook his head. Namsilat poured the black stone out into his hand.

"WHRRR! That is a true Hydra's heart is it not? My people…" Ish had started to say, when Namsilat handed him the stone.

"I had given it to your people, and those butchers slaughtered every one of them and stole it. They were the ones I tracked to Sandy. There is at least one more of them as well, and now that I know they are in the city, I must finish my debt."

"In good time, for now I must insist that you pocket your revenge and join me for a meal and good wine. I know of a family that I can pass this down to; they will see that it is put to good purpose. It is a rare man who gives such a strong gift once, but to do it twice speaks of your blood, my friend. Come, we go to the Inner Curtain.

"The Castle?" Namsilat asked.

"No, it's a shady little inn I know…of course, the Castle!" Ish turned and headed back into the main street. Turning north he led Namsilat up the stone roadway that led to the Gatehouse, behind it sat the towering pinnacles of Castle Coeur D'Alene, home of the

King and royal family. Namsilat had never seen the Kingdom, now he was being told he would be entering its Castle. Ish must either know the guards or he really was the great magician he professed to be.

The Gatehouse guards met the pair as they approached. Namsilat figured this was where the payoff would take place.

"Good day, Master Ish! Here for the celebration?" One of the men called out as he saluted the Gnome.

"That I am, my good fellow. Are you all taking the night off to folly and chase the wenches?"

"Nay to that, I am afraid. We have been put on double watch that night sir, perhaps you could speak to…"

"I will put in a good word for you gentlemen. Has a message come for me? I was expecting…"

"Expect not, my little friend. I have come in person. It has been too long to send parchment to meet such an old friend. Enter."

Namsilat stared at the man as he approached. He was exactly as the legend has told; short, heavy-set, his hair slick and shiny as if it were melted to his head, which in fact it was rumored to be. The skin-tight red leather armor fit so perfectly it looked as if it were his natural skin.

"Doro?" Namsilat felt the earth beneath his knee before he realized he had knelt.

"Rise, child, do I know you?" the high priest asked as he approached the kneeling man.

"No, but, but I know of you and…"

"Ah yes the legend. I do hope Ish here has not given you the Gnomish version, I guess you're not really old enough to have heard that rendition. Stand up and let me see you." Doro stood reaching out an open hand to Namsilat.

As Namsilat stood he could feel the scrutinizing eyes of truth penetrate his being. Why would Doro, High Priest of Thor, be using such powers on him?

"You seem an honest enough fellow, but one can never judge by first impressions." He took Namsilat's hand and gave him a welcoming shake. "I have prepared the table as you asked; it may take a little while for us to all assemble. There has been much fuss over this kid's birthday, you know. Entrance to the Inner Curtain has been strictly reduced; your message stirred a lot of thoughts, old friend. I am afraid that too good of news, spurs suspicion in some."

"As it did in me; at first, but I have since seen much to relieve those suspicions. Walk ahead with me a moment, my old friend, so that we might speak in private."

The two stepped rapidly ahead of Namsilat. He did his best to fall back, but his legs out measured both of theirs by two. He turned a deaf ear to their conversation, for he had heard Ish mention a private talk and be he a lot of things, rude he was not. He followed the men up the rampart towards the inner gate. Without hesitation they marched passed the guards; Namsilat still felt uncertain of his place and eyed the guards nervously, half expecting them to stop him. Through the gate the inner courtyard opened into a vast arena, to his right laid the entrance to the stables. He could smell the fresh roses in bloom above the archway. The King's garden lay to his left, fifty-plus yards of reds, yellows, purples and blues. Tall shrubs lined the outer perimeter framing the whole thing in deep shades of green. A huge circular walkway separated the courtyard from the marble steps that led up to the castle doors. He could feel his heart pick up its pace as his companions turned and started across the walkway. "Were they really going into the Castle?" Rude or no, he could not see himself entering the Castle this far behind the others. He stepped up closer.

"...and I say it is an omen... Oh my boy" Doro changed the subject "...a bit overwhelming I imagine" he offered in understanding as they cleared the walkway. Doro gestured for Namsilat to go ahead of them. "You are welcome here my child, I assure you."

Namsilat's eyes scanned the ever-rising towers that marked the four corners of the outer walls of the stronghold. They rose up from the ground some hundred or more feet, each topped with a metal tent to prevent the rains from falling into them. The front wall measured a good two hundred feet from tower to tower. The walls were constructed of huge stones, and then covered in mortar to give them extra strength. There were three large windows facing the courtyard, one every twenty feet, parallel up the front of each tower. Namsilat assumed them to be separate floors of the great mansion. In the center of these huge walls rested a great staircase. Forty steps made of solid marble and laid in place by master masons, leading to the grand doors, thirty feet high, dark Mahogany, a foot thick, polished iron framed the edges and across centers of each door. As the doormen swung them open, Namsilat's eyes strained to see the length of the huge room inside.

"Go on boy, you can see it much better from the inside." Doro urged him to continue walking.

Namsilat stepped through the wide entryway and listened as his footstep echoed down and came back. The room opened under a forty foot cathedral-style ceiling, spiral staircases leading up from the center and along the right and left sides of the main hall. The flags and banners of every lord in the realm hung off walkways running the full length of the second floor. Suits of armor lined the main floor from the entrance to the first of three visible inner walls, separating it into four sections. Tapestries and paintings hung along the walls behind them giving the room an almost crowded feeling. The great ceiling was a painted mural, depicting what he could only guess was the great battle that ended the dark times. Namsilat's awe was only surpassed by his Elvin repulsion to the waste of the land that had to occur for this structure to exist.

"Not a bad little getaway, hey?" Ish's voice announced.

"Not if you're human, I guess." Namsilat answered.

The Gnome and the Dwarf broke into a heart-felt laughter. Namsilat followed their lead as they turned towards the right staircase. Reaching the far wall, Master Doro mumbled something Namsilat could not quite makes sense of. A spell he figured, as the wall before them began grinding and slid to the left opening up a doorway into the wall itself.

"I hope you are hungry, boy." Ish spoke as they entered the dark passageway.

Doro led the way. Namsilat's eyes slowly began to adjust to the darkness, and he could tell that the walls were only a few feet apart and that the passageway slanted downward at a very slow and deceiving rate. There was fresh air coming from ahead of them, although he could see no sign of light indicating any openings. They walked a short while. Doro mumbled again, and again the darkness was replaced by a large well-lit chamber on the other side of a secret wall.

"Is it wise to sneak around in a castle?" Namsilat asked in jest as they entered what appeared to be a dining room of sorts. He could hear music coming from somewhere up ahead of them, and the sounds of laughter began touching his ears.

"We are no longer in the castle, my good fellow. We are at one of the finest eateries in all of Coeur D'Alene." Doro offered as they cleared a second wall. Welcome to Clappers Inn, where the prices are high, but then so are the clients."

Suddenly they were in a room filled with very well-to-do nobles. People laughed and drank, a Bard played away on a small stage at the far end of the tables. There were several barmaids running food and drink from table to table. Namsilat could smell honeyed pig, roasted potatoes and garlic, mutton, veal, beef and even pheasant. There was the sweet smell of Elvin wine and the rot of Dwarven ale. The tables were all full, save one at the edge of the stage. Doro and Ish pointed for him to sit there and they would fetch food and drink.

As Namsilat approached the stage, the Bard finished the song he had been reciting. He took up his lute and began playing. The crowd settled into a lower pitched drone as he softened the tempo. Ish and Doro were now making their way back through the center of the crowd towards the table. Several of the barmaids started picking up plates they had just sat down, Namsilat watched a few moments and noticed some of the patrons were putting up a little fuss. He saw one of the maids point in the direction of the Priest as he reached the table. Without any further hesitation, they stood and departed.

"Seems as if no one wants to eat with us" Namsilat jousted.

"I have asked for a little privacy, I hope you don't mind." Doro fenced back.

"No, not at all. I prefer a quiet meal." The Bard fell silent and he turned to see what had happened. A barmaid was pointing at the trio and whispering to the man, who quickly stood and walked off behind the curtain. When all was quiet, he heard the rumble of something heavy being drug across the wooden floor, but his eyes perceived nothing. Another spell he guessed.

"What no music?" he touted.

"We have something a little more appropriate for this evening's entertainment, lad." Ish responded this time. As he spoke a pair of women approached the table carrying huge platters of food.

"Ah our meal." Doro and Ish wasted no time digging into the stuffed piglet and potato dressing on the first platter. Their munching and grunting almost disturbed the younger man. The second platter contained a huge Salmon baked and filleted exposing the bright pink flesh Namsilat detested. Too many of his trail meals had consisted of such a main course. He reached in and grabbed a leg off the suckling and a hunk of bread off the platter now being delivered. Wine and ale came as well, and the three devoured the meal as if they had not eaten in days. Soon the burping began. Doro let loose and Ish

followed. Namsilat did not know for sure what was going on, but he

was here. If there was going to be trouble, he at least wanted to enjoy

these brief moments with this legend of a Dwarf. Reaching across

the table for more bread, Namsilat noticed a figure enter behind

Doro and Ish through what he figured was the front door.

The man wore the hood of his cloak up, to hide his face. He

took the bread and leaned back. Doro and Ish seemed less than

alarmed as the man took up a seat at the table across from them.

"There goes the neighborhood." Doro grunted, spitting food

and ale upon the table as he spoke.

"I'll say." Ish added.

Barroom brawling was never Namsilat's thing, and why

these two well-versed men would start one so blatantly, was beyond

his comprehension. But much of this day was starting to go that way.

He quickly scanned the room; there were three visible exits. The one

they had come through, although now re-concealed, though once an

Elf sees a door, it always sees the door. The second was as he had guessed, the main door, for now another figure came through it, concealing his identity under a hood as well. This one was a shade taller than the first, but both were built slight of body and carried themselves very surely. The third exit would be through the kitchen doorway. Not visible, but he would bet it was there.

The second figure sat down at the table next to the first, they neither spoke nor looked at each other. Namsilat took a closer look as he leaned in for the wine bottle between him and Ish. He thought maybe they were his friends from Sandy. But the first one was an Elf. Even hooded his features spoke for themselves. The second man was probably human; his posture did not speak to the elegance with which all Elves carried themselves. Namsilat heard the grinding sound of something heavy moving again across the floor, this time it was more distinct and he could tell it was coming from the area around the stage.

"So my lad, Ish tells me, you have little respect for your father. Seems getting one's self killed on the field of battle is not honorable enough for you?" Doro's statement caused him to choke a little, his eyes focused on the mage.

"My issue with my father really seems to be none of your concern, Master Doro." Namsilat's mood declined even faster as Ish coughed and spat food at him, slapping Doro across the shoulder.

"I guess he told you."

"I see no humor here. I was invited here under the guise of kinship, only to be accosted for my personal business. I bid you good day, gentlemen." Namsilat began to stand only to find that his chair was being held very securely against the wall by Lord Doro's booted foot. "I have no fight with you good sir. If you wish to hold me here to further assault me, I must warn…"

"Warn me not, lad. I will let you go as you wish, but I would first have a word. Perhaps I am too blunt; let me rephrase my statement. Ish tells me that there is bad blood between you and your father, but that you never really met the man you hold in such contempt." Doro eyes poised a question.

"My father and my relationship, or lack thereof, is still none of your concern, no matter how you 'phrase' it! Now I would that you should remove your foot." Namsilat was confused by the sudden change in the two men. He felt the pressure of Doro's boot lighten, and he pushed back from the table to stand. A bright light to his left caught him unaware momentarily and the Talon flashed into his hand.

"I told you he was kindred." Ish announced, pointing at the glowing blade.

"And so I see he may be," Doro conceded. Both men looked at the sword now glowing in Namsilat's hand. He looked down and quickly sheathed the weapon.

"I, must apolo…"

"Apologize not, lad. I am an old fool, and I fear I am at an awkward spot here. My intentions were not to alarm you in any way. I simply want to enlighten you a little."

"If this is about how my hatred for a man I do not know can sour me and eat me from the inside, then save your breath. I have spent the last two years in the company of many who have sung that song, over and over. I know the folly of my anger, and it is only in times like these, where I am asked by people who neither know me or the man I choose to despise..."

"You assume much my young man, for I know more than you think on both matters." Doro's words gave him pause.

CHAPTER 9

The curtain on the stage now rattled as it was drawn open by unseen hands. Namsilat turned and watched as the curtain parted to reveal five figures standing in the center of the stage. They stood motionless and Namsilat slowly began to recognize them. He stepped closer peering in curiosity at the lifeless, life-size figures of the King's Riders. They were in the same order as the ones at the fountain. Moyie stood far right facing the bar, Bonner to his left, in front of him to the right Master Doro, then Hea'fxtrot, all behind the figure of King Darrin. Unlike the fountain, these figures were in full color, not cold white stone. Had Lord Doro not been standing in front of him at this moment, he would swear it was him on the stage. Each wore a green fur cloak pinned with an amulet of silver and gold. Namsilat looked at Doro and Ish.

"What sort of illusion is this?"

"It is not an illusion; they are made of a sort of molding wax. The King had them fashioned as a model for the fountain makers. When the fountain was finished he had them brought here and preserved. Many travelers come here just to view them." Doro informed him.

Namsilat scanned the waxen statues again. The detail was amazing. They had real hair, and their clothing he could tell was real as well. In front of Doro's likeness stood the great hammer of Thor, a gift from his God to a faithful servant. Yet Master Doro also held the hammer now in the bar.

"And their weapons are they wax as well?"

"No, they are exact replicas of those carried into the battle." Doro answered.

The matching dual swords of Moyie Spring, the double-edged blade that served Bonner for so long, rumored to have been buried with him in a watery funeral by his friends after he fell. The Armor of the Planes, white hot and impenetrable by any earthly blade, fashioned by the legendary Lawrence Smithy donned by King Darrin, the six-wand staff of Hea'fxtrot, a most chaotic creation, forged in times of great desperation. Around the neck of each man, save that of Bonner, hung a golden chain, Namsilat stepped up onto the stage to take a closer look. Reaching out with his left hand he lifted the coin around the neck of Doro's figure, not quite sure if touching the figure of a King was like that of touching a real King. Holding the silver and gold charm he saw the sword and holly leaf on a blue sapphire backing. Turning it over he found the inscription he had come to know by heart. 'Forever Bound'! He staggered back away from the figures and off the stage.

When he turned, he was met by the gaze of Ish and Doro. The other two men had stepped alongside of them, their hoods now pulled back to reveal their faces. On the right stood Moyie Spring, the greatest Elfin Ranger to ever live, and to his left Hea'fxtrot, Shaman and now ruler of the WarmSpring Peoples.

"I think he is going pass out!" Moyie's voice echoed in his mind as if he were far away in a very long tunnel.

"What is this, why, it cannot be, I, my mother never…"

"She thought it best for you, at the time, and that decision was hers to make, not ours. Your being Half-blood was going to make your life hard enough she figured, and the Half-blood child of a hero, would be even harder to live with." Moyie offered.

"But it can't be. My father died in the war?"

"And that he did Lad, but not the war you thought he died in. He lived through that one and was returning to you and your mother when we…"

"When they stopped to help a foolish farm boy save a maiden." The firm voice came from behind the group. As they stepped aside, Namsilat's eyes fell upon the King, his knee bent and he knelt.

"Oh please, raise Namsilat Ferrie, I ask none of these men, nor shall I ask you to hold me in any reverence when we are in private. Let me look at you."

Namsilat stood on trembling legs, the conversation going on around him made his head spin.

"He looks a lot like his father. Did your mother ever tell you that?"

"No, she said..."

"Has his father's temper too, should have seen him draw on the old one there." Moyie jested.

"I thought he was going to get nasty there for a heartbeat or two." Hea'fxtrot offered, giving a nod. The men all jested and laughed as Namsilat tried to take it all in. The barmaids returned with food and more wine. The food and drink helped his head clear a little but then they began telling stories, of the war, the black mage and of his father, Bonner Ferrie.

"Remember down in Zigzag when Hea'fxtrot threw that hornets' nest into that inn. Man, what a ruckus that caused." Moyie teased

"I believe that was your King that did that." Hea'fxtrot countered.

"Oh, no you don't. You know full well whose deed that was." Darrin interjected. And they burst into laughter again.

******

After many hours of food and drink, the mood settled into one of somberness. King Darrin looked over at the confused, and now a little drunken, Namsilat.

"So, do you have any questions of us, my boy?" Doro grumbled out.

"I would not know where to begin, my lord. I have spent all these years hating and revering the same man and never gave much thought to the idea that he was one in the same. My mother was right in not telling me. A secret is easier to keep if you do not know it. But I would have liked to have had a hint, maybe, or even a last name. But all in all, mother was wiser than her years and I hold no contempt to her. Why had none of you come to find us?"

"I stopped by twice, the last time was at a festival near your village. I was beginning to tell you that I was your father's friend, when I noticed your mother coming. The fire exploded, you looked away and I made my escape." Moyie began.

"That was you? All these years I thought it his ghost."

Again they all laughed.

"No, I am quite sure that your father would never haunt you. He loved your mother very much and you as well. I spoke to your mother that night and offered to take you with me. I was returning home and told her you would be welcome there. She thought not. You had already begun to handle the names and were quite big about it, so she did not wish to have you go hide somewhere and start all over. She knew it would be just as hard amongst the Elves, I'd guess. I offered to send you a tutor to train you in the arts of fighting and hunting, but again she thought you were getting along just fine. And I see you have!" Moyie glanced down at his sword.

"Like so much of my life I guess, I stumbled upon this retched gift as well." Namsilat raised the Talon and tossed it on the table.

"How so, young Ferrie? Honor us with tales of how one comes by a Kindred Blade by stumble and folly!" Doro raised his tankard, tossed his booted feet up on the table, and leaned back as one would do when listening to a Bard's tale.

"My folly would seem quiet unimpressive to the likes of you fellows I am afraid, my good Dwarf." Namsilat did not feel the boast in him that he had always relished when given a chance to speak of his favorite topic.

"Oh please young friend…we are old washed-up adventurers, long from the trail and overwrought with regret. It is only through the tales of others we ever get out of these binds of rank and position." Darrin offered.

"Speak not for me, my confined friend. I live a life of excitement and danger almost daily. Just yesterday I was called to bless a new warrior as he started his life as a member of the great WarmSpring people, in no less than thirteen seasons he will even be old enough to hunt." Hea'fxtrot teased.

"I actually got to spend time with the great adventuring group of the Wemme Brothers just this morning," Doro added. The group all began to laugh and lean to Namsilat for a tale. He held out as long as he could, then he began sharing his miss-luck of the fateful discovery and the demise of Astre. Just as he was getting to the battle on the ice field, Doro's snoring drowned him out… looking around the table he could see that the wine and the ale had taken its toll on all, save Moyie.

"They shall regret not hearing the end of your tale, my friend. As for I, it is an honor to know one who can share not only his victory, but the honesty of his fears. Your father is proud." Moyie raised a glass of wine to toast.

"You and Bonner…my father, were close the tales say." Namsilat returned the toast.

"That we were. We set out from Osoyoos Valley, where we were born, and we crossed over into the human realm and found ourselves adventure and…folly. It was from one such folly Bonner, your father and my dearest friend, lost his life. We had been in service to the last King's army, we had helped chase the Orcs back into the southern boundaries and were on our way home when we met Darrin and found ourselves locked in a battle far graver than any we had encountered in the war. We could not just turn our backs on the humans and go home; the evil that was rising in their lands would soon have come for us there as well. We made the choice to stay and fight."

"And all our peoples are indebted to them for that decision." Darrin rose, toasted the pair, drank down the last of his tankard and bowed. "I fear I must leave you, my friends. My bride does not allow me to stay out of her chambers for a full night, unless there is war… and for today there is no war." He gave a bow then turned to Namsilat. "As is for all these who rode with me, and was for your father, passed to you by rite of birth - my home, my lands and all I have are yours should you ever find need of anything. Thank the Gods and Goddess we have found you. He gave another bow and staggered out through the hidden passage.

"This is so…" Namsilat began to say.

"It is too much to try to reason in a night, Namsilat. Give yourself and your mind time to let it in. If your hatred for your estranged father is to heal, like any wound it will take time. Do not think that we demand anything from you. When your mother passed I offered to keep track of you, but Darrin saw fit that you should come to us if it were the will of the Gods, and now it would seem that it is. Our only hope is that we can somehow be of service to you. Know this, you owe us nothing and we hold you to nothing. If you choose to embrace your father as we knew him, so be it. If, however, the years and pain are too strong, know that we judge not. He was our friend. We lost him. But he was your father and you never got to know him. For that we bear a share of burden." Moyie gave a slight bow.

"It's just...I mean I never thought...mother never said and I guess I always wished that you or Bonner, were my father. Not some loser that ran out on his wife and child to die for...what? I never heard that he was in the Black War; just that he had died fighting with humans. She never even mentioned any of you."

"She feared...and rightfully so, that we may have stolen you away as well, my young friend. You were the only connection she had left to the man she loved with all her heart. We will speak more on this I am certain, but for tonight, try to get some rest. Darrin's mood concerns me. I fear the fates, or the Gods, depending on your view, may have brought you here as a sign of more than happy reunions." Moyie offered his hand. As the two men shook, Doro

snored louder, causing them to laugh. "You look just like him you

know? Goodnight, Namsilat Ferrie." Moyie turned and walked out.

CHAPTER 10

Earlier that Day

Built five hundred years before his birth, Coeur D'Alene castle was all young E'rik had been told was left of the vast homeland his father ruled. "Adventuring is for peasants and the dissatisfied" his protective mother had told him as a youth. "I'll not have my son out wandering the wilds as animal bait!" She would scold his father every time he even suggested that the boy might enjoy a trip to such far away and exotic places as Na'ple or PortsLand. Had it not been for the band of Brothers Four, and his father's willingness to turn a blind eye once in a while, so that the young Prince could break free from studying, it would be all he ever knew.

He looked down from his balcony. Everywhere there were banners and flags announcing that he was of age. There was to be a great celebration in his honor. A ball would be held and young women from every city, town and hamlet would come to vie for his affection. Servants raced around on the grounds below him, cleaning and butchering, all in preparation for the party he so desperately wanted to miss. The Brothers were out there somewhere near the Mount Hood, scaling the heights and fighting beasts most of these people had never even heard of, enjoying camp fire meals with charcoal in every bite, the smell of sweaty horses and clanging of swords as you fought for your very life. Chance encounters with fair maidens that would woo you because of your charms, not because of your father's station. Three young boys took flight after a pack of chickens, their mother screaming for them to stop; they disappeared into the alley out of his sight. Oh, to be them, just for another day, carefree, duty free, happy go lucky.

"What has you so preoccupied this day my, young Prince?" Doro's voice broke the spell as he entered the Prince's chamber.

"Oh! Master Doro. I did not hear you knocking.

"That is because I did not knock E'rik. I saw you from the courtyard. I could not help but notice that you were here but off in the distance as well. Where is your mind off to this day?" The Dwarf entered and placed himself on the footstool at E'rik's side.

"Anywhere, really, other than locked in my chambers awaiting the arrival of people who only know me because my father is the King."

"Is it not good to be heir to the throne?" the wise old Dwarf teased. He had been a wanderer himself for many years. It was only duty to his King and service to his God that had kept him here these past twenty years. He knew all too well the blood that surged through the young man's veins, for he had ridden with King Darrin, the boy's father, and E'rik was his true heir. Castles and kingdoms held little appeal to the boy's father either. But he had accepted his place and done very well by his people. But there were many a night when Doro and the King had bantered of times passed and Darrin's wish for freedom.

"What if I did not want to be heir? What if I wanted to be a soldier, or a scout for new lands? Wandering here and there, seeking out new adventures and treasures for the King's vault, fighting alongside other men in the field of battle, protecting the Kingdom from invaders." The young fair-haired boy waltzed around, fencing shadows and smiling.

"Oh, this one has it bad." The old Dwarf thought to himself

"Why can't we have a war...?" E'rik blurted out.

"Now, hold your tongue right there, E'rik. Of adventuring I understand, but by the Gods and the faithful works of your father and many others, this kingdom has not known war for over twenty years. I for one do not wish it so, and you would be wise not to arouse the desires of the fates. You know nothing of war; I have been through two of them and do not hope to see a third before I pass on. War is a horrible thing, both good and bad suffer. It does not save its ravages for those who deserve them. No, young Prince, you would do well to hope that you never see a war." The old Dwarf was stern in his response. Looking for adventure was one thing; war was a whole different story and not one he wanted to relive.

"But father and you tell of the great men, the battles and heroes."

"Your father and I share the good times with you. Perhaps a more honest revelation would be of the fallen comrades, the desolated homes and farms, the horrible destruction raining down on

106

women and children as they flee from their homes and villages. The smells of the burning carcasses and rotting dead would be better stories to tell. These are the parts of war you try to forget, you create festivals and dedicate days in remembrance of those whom you loved and lost. These are the ways you try to heal, my young Prince; it is not good to have a day named after you. It means you are dead!" With that the old Dwarf stood and turned away from the boy.

"Your father has asked me to prepare a blessing for your birth gift. I think I shall pray you be relieved of these foolish ideas. I am too old now to return to war, and you are too young to have to fight. Now get dressed. I have something to show you."

E'rik rushed to dress; he had always enjoyed master Doro's gifts. As he wandered down the huge spiraling staircase to the main floor of the castle, he scanned the hall for Doro.

"Good day master E'rik" Anna called as she passed him on the stairs.

"Have you seen Master Doro, Anna?"

"I believe he was in the reading room near the library, Sire," the maid offered.

"Thank you!" He rushed on skipping the last three stairs.

"Master E'rik, please be more careful. If your mother..." The head butler called out.

"But my mother did not see me. Have you seen Master Doro, Rondal?"

"I believe he was entertaining some gentlemen out in the courtyard, Sire." The butler offered.

"Thank you!" The Prince shouted back as he rushed towards the main doors of the Castle. The doormen swung the huge, iron-framed, Mahogany panels open as the young Prince approached.

"Master Doro, have you seen him?"

"Around in the stables young sire." One of the doormen offered, pointing towards the riding area to the left of the front stairs.

E'rik rushed down the forty granite steps that led to the entrance of the Castle. His feet barely touched down before he took off to the stables.

"DORO! Master Doro, are you out here?" He called as he rushed through the huge gates separating the riding area from the main courtyard. Large yellow rose bushes grew up the sides and over the archway, trimming the dark oak gate in soft pastels. E'rik's heart was racing as he cleared the edge of the stable house and entered the arena. There was a moment of silence as he looked around the open dirt ring, seeing nothing but the stable boy raking the dirt.

"Have you seen Lord Doro?" E'rik called out as he approached the young lad. All the boy did was glance towards an open stable door at the far end of the barn. E'rik took to running, clearing the fifty yards in seconds. As his eyes began to see the inside of the open stable his ears rang. A most offensive attempt at trumpeting screamed at him as the brothers emerged from inside the wooden structure. Percy blew again, his second attempt was worse than his first, if that were possible. E'rik's hands shot to his ears in defense.

"What in the Gods names are you four doing here?"

"We have come to celebrate your birth with you and we have brought, what we hope, will be your finest gift."

The four had been standing shoulder to shoulder across the front of the stable doors, while behind then a white horse bobbed its head from time to time. E'rik had assumed it was one of the visitor's mounts. But as Tom announced the gift, the brothers parted like swinging doors and behind them stood Doro, holding the reigns to his new friend.

"They say they acquired it by rightful means my Lord, but a finer beast I have never seen and I doubt that these four, with their luck in adventuring, could afford such fine horse flesh." Doro offered as the young Prince approached.

She was a beautiful creature, eyes as blue as sapphires, her coat as white as virgin snow. She stood fifteen hands; her mane had been braided with baby's breath and ruby red roses from the garden.

She held her head high and proud, sniffing this new stranger as E'rik came in and rubbed gently under her chin. Her tail shot up like the fountains at festival time. She was full of spirit and seemed to approve of him as much as he did her. With a swift firm motion, she nudged the young man's cheek, giving him an accepting kiss as it were.

"She is beautiful!" was about all he could say. His hands drifted up over her nose, scratching gently as they made their way between her velvety ears, and then down her soft braided mane. His right arm swung up under her neck and he patted down along her throat as he walked slowly along her side, giving her a gentle but firm slap on the rump, then petting her back to her head and nuzzling her huge cheek.

"What shall I call you girl?" he looked deep into her eyes searching for a signal as he offered up a name. "Sapphire!" Her eyes twinkled and she blinked.

"She is the only child of the breeding of a true Unicorn and a Pegasus; she has the spirit of her mother and runs like her father flies. I would wager on her in any race in any kingdom. She is sure-footed and steady; her lungs could carry you from here to PortsLand at full speed. And despite what the good Priest says, our adventuring these last two seasons has been grand. Oh if you could have only been with us up the Mount Hood E'rik!" Tom began to boast Percy nudged him to silence.

"What?"

"You know he wanted to go. Now let him enjoy his gift without your babblings." Shade cut in as he joined E'rik by the horse. "She is a thing of grand beauty and fitting for a Prince. I hope she takes you far and fast, young E'rik."

The two friends shook hands, as they pulled each other in for a hug. E'rik noticed over Shades shoulder that the other three brothers and Lord Doro had taken to their knees. He had begun to rib them while turning around, fully expecting to find his father there.

"Since when do the brothers bow to my…"

His mouth fell silent as quickly as his eyes settled on his mother. Although Queen of Coeur D'Alene, Sulaunna had not lost her true nature. She was a rogue through and through and today she wore her favorite fitted, blood-red leather armor, a gift from her loving husband the King.

"Good morning, Mother, I sort of expected…"

"Your father, his Majesty, is in chambers with some of his border guards. I heard that these fellows of yours had arrived and I just want to make clear that you are not to take off with these hooligans!" She passed an almost serious glance over the brothers.

"We would never…"Tom began to speak.

"Yes, you would, Sir Thomas. And do not think for a moment that his father could, or would for that matter; be able to protect you should you abscond with my son on his birthday. We all know too well what you gentlemen are capable of, and for this one occasion I must insist that you respect my wishes." The Queen turned to face them.

"Yes Your Highness." The band chirped up. E'rik and his mother could not help but burst into laughter.

"I am grateful that you were able to make it here for my son's celebration." As she spoke her eyes fell upon the mare standing beside Shade.

"Oh my, what a magnificent creature she is." The Queen stepped forward and placed a knowing hand on the animal's snout. "Where did you find her?" she glanced at the group.

"We actually had her made just for this occasion. She is two years old the very same day E'rik turns twenty. It was all my idea." Tom bragged.

"Yeah right, more like you were the only one resisting spending the coin on her!" Percy offered back.

"Not that I doubt your sincerity Tom, but I am inclined to trust Sir Percy." With her announcement the party all began to laugh. Sulaunna smiled at Tom trying his best to look boyish. It seemed she knew him all too well.

"May I take her for a ride, mother? "The young Prince pleaded.

Rubbing the mane of the beautiful creature, Sulaunna smiled at her young son. "It would seem an awful waste to keep her all saddled up and indoors. I guess a short ride could not hurt. But mark my words Brothers Four; it is two days till the festival in celebration of my son's birth begins. He is to be back in these walls and accounted for before the crowing of the cock on that second day. If he is not, I swear I shall have you all in the dungeon by that nightfall. Do you understand me?" Her voice became very stern as she looked around the group, eyeing each in turn.

"Our oath to you, my Lady, we will keep him no more than a day." Tom offered.

"And do not bring him home smelling of cheap wine or bar wenches!"

"Indeed Your Highness, it will be only the finest of either. You sully our good reputation with such talk." Shade offered as he and the others left to retrieve their horses.

"Thank you mother, I will return safe and sane for the celebration." E'rik said as he embraced his mother. When he began to pull away her arms tightened around his shoulders.

"E'rik, there is talk of trouble coming to our lands, I want you to be extra careful. Your father would not soon forgive either of us should anything happen to you."

"What sort of trouble, mother?"

"I do not know for certain, your father is mostly keeping it from me. He says he does not want me to worry. And you are not to tell him that we have spoken on this matter. His ambassadors have been bringing reports to him these past few weeks. Whatever it is it has your father concerned and that concerns me. Now you stay close to these fellows, she raised her voice slightly as the brothers returned; cannon fodder is no good if it is behind you." With that she released his arm and glanced up at Tom.

"Fodder? Is that what we've become?"Tom objected. E'rik nudged Sapphire out in front of him.

"Be glad. There was a time that her words for you did not hold any use." He kicked Sapphire giving her the go ahead and she took flight. He could hear the other brothers cheering their mounts on as he sped away leaving poor Tom in dismay.

CHAPTER 11

The gatemen opened the portcullis as E'rik and Sapphire bore down on the gatehouse. With his long golden hair blowing behind him, the young prince shouted out his freedom as he shot out the other side of the castle wall.

"Yahoo!" Giving Sapphire another kick, he brought her to a full run down the main street leading into the township. People dove off the dirt and stone roadway, making room for the crazed rider, many unaware that it was the Prince. Shouts of displeasure met the trailing band as the brothers emerged from the gatehouse.

"Fools, these roads are too crowded for such folly." A man shouted out as they passed.

"You're going to kill someone, idiot!" Pedestrians shook their fists as the brothers struggled to catch up with the young Prince, now a good hundred yards ahead of them. Sapphire had not even gotten in her stride. She was holding back until the Prince gave her the command.

E'rik cleared the upper quarter in no time. Pressing down on the town square he was faced with a decision. South would lead him out into the main courtyard of the city; from there it was two-hundred feet to the main wall. Through those gates lay the open valley known as Coeur D'Alene, a land as rich in history as it was fertile in soil. To the east lay the Bad Lands, uncharted and unexplored after the first full day's journey. Somewhere beyond that marker lay the Castle Dominic; one of E'rik's fathers greatest rivals. He and the brothers had ventured onto Dominic's land a few times, but since their run-in with some scouts, they had thought it better not to provoke a war, just for the sake of adventure. To the west, ah, that is where E'rik's heart truly laid, the rolling mountains and open clear-blue skies. Snow covered mountain peaks and valleys full of life. Rivers filled to overflowing with trout and the giant salmon, the elk herds that ran from the upper border of the great Columbia River to the desserts of Re'dMond. This is where the jeweled city of PortsLand lay and that is where E'rik hoped to make his new home after the celebration.

He had not mentioned any of this to his father or mother. It would be his surprise to them after his birthday. A sudden shout and Sapphire's quick jerk to the right brought his attention back to the moment. He had all but run down a man and a small oddly dressed child, crossing in front of the city fountain; the man made a grab for the small child, which vanished before the Prince's eyes, sending the man sprawling across the ground at the fountains base. The fountain was a monument to the riders of his father's first campaign against the enemies of King Erik, E'rik's namesake. It stood in the center of the City Square, twenty-five feet high and forty feet at the base Granite statues of the now 'King Darrin' and his four companions. E'rik held tight to the reins as Sapphire lunged hard to avoid hitting the screaming man. His knees grabbed hold of her sides to keep from taking an early morning swim in the fountain. Sapphire tossed back to the left and it appeared the fates had decided on south. E'rik urged her on and the city guards rushed to open the huge gates as the Prince flew towards them with no apparent intent on slowing, let alone stopping. The brothers made the fountain just as E'rik cleared the gate, breaking out into the open roadway leading to the villages and farms scattered across the Coeur D'Alene countryside. E'rik sat straight in the saddle, turning to shout over his shoulders.

"Hooray! I am free for the day. You had better catch up, or I shall have to return before you have even left, my brothers." He taunted the band as they slapped leather to their mounts in hopes of at least keeping him in sight.

"Do you think we should give him the command word?" Percy asked as he came along Tom's side.

"Not in the Hells, my good fellow, not till we return." They took to laughing as they pushed their horses harder.

The Brothers pressed to catch up with young E'rik as he barreled down the dirt road, his hands raised to either side, his cloak flapping in the wind behind him as he stood in the stirrups praising his freedom. He could smell the fresh spring flowers blooming all around. Life was blossoming everywhere, newborn animals raced around discovering their new world, the smell of fresh turned soil waiting to be planted with the fruits for fall harvest. E'rik loved nature and all her beauty, being locked away even for a short time made him feel dead. The Castle and all its charms were not for him. He was meant for adventure and now after his birthday, he could set out and no one could stop him. A journey to the forbidden lands perhaps, or up into the great northlands of Ice Dragons and the Yeti. His mind raced on as Tom pulled alongside of him.

"We had hoped that you might be in need of a little break, young Prince. Shade thought that maybe a good run out to the village of Hayden, then up along the Great Crater back into the Kingdom. We thought we might stay by a lake; do a little fishing then stop by Marybeth's Inn sometime tomorrow. But you cannot tell your mother we took you there, no bragging around to the servants either. You know how word spreads inside castle walls."

"My friend, you have no idea how grand it is to be outside again. Mother has insisted that I remain close these last few months. Winter was too mild and father seemed to be worried that there might be trouble from Dominic's people raiding the smaller villages in the south region." E'rik breathed in the fresh air as the other brothers began catching up.

"So where are we off to, Master E'rik?" Percy asked as he rode up alongside.

"Just E'rik, Percy. I hate the title stuff, it is too restraining. And out here I feel more like a person than a Prince. Tom was saying we should head over to Hayden."

"Sounds good I hear they have been having a lot of bear trouble, maybe we could even get in on a hunt?"

"Bear hunt?" E'rik's excitement was obvious.

"Yes, it seems the creatures have been making off with small dogs. I have heard that there are a couple of children missing as well." Percy continued.

"How do you get this information, Percy?" Shade asked as he closed in on the group, Al'daLane, was at his flank.

"Oh, I have my ways. One must keep abreast of all things going on around the realms, if one is to be a successful adventurer." The group took to laughing as they rode on towards the split that would take them further southeast towards Hayden.

Tom and E'rik caught up on Tom's favorite topic, himself, while the rest of the small band fell back a few yards and rode in silence for most of the way to the split. At the fork, they turned right and began the five-hour journey that would lead them down into Hayden. They slowed to an easier pace for the rest of the mounts;

though Sapphire showed no hint of the run they had just been on. The lack of any real snow, but lots of rain, had taken its toll on the mud roadway. Deep ruts and a few boulders that had fallen off the edge of the embankments made the going slow and arduous.

An hour into their journey Shade rode up and pointed out the old mining road off to their left and suggested they take the trail that led down across the valley floor, rather than continuing along the road. It was less traveled and he had not been down that trail in many years. E'rik had never even seen the old Dwarven mines that were abandoned after King Darefiet, his great-grandfather, had conquered the realm and established Coeur d'Alene. They all agreed that it might be a nice break from road travel so they took the overgrown trailhead and started down the steep trail into the forgotten valley.

The trail was much smaller than the road; it made for single file riding most of the time. To their right was the muddy hillside lined with evergreens and scrub Oak trees doing their best to wrestle out life anywhere their roots could lay hold. The steep embankment was spotted with jagged rocks and trees that had fallen in the heavy rains. The left side of the trail was a gradual drop off into the valley floor. From their saddles they caught glimpses of the huge meadow that lay some hundred feet below them.

Sapphire paused as a covey of game birds chucked and took to the wing just in front of her. E'rik patted her ears and nudged her on. He had not even heard the birds until she stopped. A few yards further she paused again, a spotted fawn darted from the brush and kicked and pranced as it raced for cover on the far side of the trail. Its mother leaped over the trail behind it and they disappeared into the thick brush, crashing their way down towards the meadow and fresh greens. Resting in eternal abandon, the old Dwarf mines came into view. The trail opened up into a small landing area where two old wagons sat, deteriorating from the elements. Pieces of old mining equipment and rotting sacks lay strewn all around the old entrance. E'rik pulled Sapphire up and began to dismount.

"Hey! What, pray tell, do you think you're doing, young Sir?" Tom called out as he raced up to the Prince.

"I thought we were going to explore the old mine."

"Not in this life span we are not. Your mother would kill us for sure, if the old mine didn't." Percy tossed in as he joined the two.

"Why?"

"Traps" Shade offered as he came into the clearing. "Lots and lots of traps I doubt if you could even get a greedy Dwarf to venture far into that tomb."

"Why would they trap an old mine?"

"It wasn't old when they trapped it. Dwarves build mines for themselves, they build them so that other Dwarves working in them can come and go unscathed. But the timbers are not always as secure as they look and the flooring can be less than sure. When they left this old mine it was because of invasion and concession, not because they were done with it." Shade continued.

"Can't you get past the traps?" the young Prince pushed on.

"We would not even ask him to. Some traps are not by passable, others cannot be disarmed. Many have ventured in over the centuries, none have returned whole. No, the treasures of this mine are not for the taking." Tom cut in.

"Surely old Shade here can see any trap." E'rik offered flattery as if to convince them.

"Not all traps are visible or actual; some traps are simple side passages, or a hint in the wrong direction. You are in them before you realize you have been taken, my young adventurer. As a rule, if

126

your guide suggests you dare not venture in, it is wise to heed his warning or why even have him along?" Shade cut him off before he got too worked up.

"A wiser statement I could not have offered." Tom added.

"I have one. Let's eat." Al'daLane had returned to the group carrying three large game birds he had used a little magic to retrieve. He climbed down off his horse and tossed them to E'rik. "Now, you do remember how to clean these things, right?"

"Why do I have to always clean the catch? I am, after all, the Prince, you know, I should…"

"Have mentioned that when you joined us not "E'rik; Percy, you know I don't like all that…………"

"Okay, Okay. I'll clean the birds, but I at least get to eat some of them this time." E'rik shouted as he took the birds up and started looking for a place to clean them.

"I'll drink to that." Tom joined in a toast, taking the wineskin then passing it around. Al'daLane made the gesture and was preparing to hand the skin back to Shade when young E'rik grabbed it.

"What about me?"

"Oh yeah, I half forgot." He teased as he released the skin.

They sat and ate the birds with bread Tom had grabbed from the kitchen. The horses were fed and rubbed down and the wine was gone. E'rik stood and headed towards the cave again moving slowly as if to ignore the others warnings.

"My Prince, where do you think you are off to?" It was the voice of a magic ward Percy had placed on the entrance.

"I was just looking." He stood a long while gazing into the darkness. Could it really be that bad, he was thinking?

"There are far greater treasures at Marybeth's for you young sire. We should be headed out if we are to reach the lake tonight." Tom's voice came from behind him.

"Do you think anything is even left in there?" E'rik asked as he turned towards Sapphire.

"No."

"Couldn't be." Three voices rang out to deter him.

"You know it. The mine was only worked for three years before the realm fell under Darefiet's rule. They barely got started." Shade offered just to antagonize the group.

"SHADE!" the others shouted in unison.

The thief laughed, as did E'rik. Mounting up they turned out onto the trail and headed for the valley below.

From the mine the trail got ugly, most of the travel was up to the road, along this path, few trips went down, usually only if an errant cart or wagon of ore went off the edge. The horses were tense as they slipped and staggered down the old muddy trail. Huge rocks lay just under the thin earthen cover of moss, which would give way under their heavy weight. Several times the riders had to wait while one or more of them fought to get back onto the trail after their horses had slipped completely off the trail into the brush. Sapphire stayed steady and sure footed the whole way; she had the grace of a ballet dancer floating across the stage as if on air. E'rik took the lead once more as they finally reached to end of the steep route.

CHAPTER 12

The trail dumped out into a huge meadow some two hundred yards long and half again as wide. The field was covered in a rainbow of spring colors from the blossoming flowers. Everywhere blues mixed with reds and yellows, purples with greens and gold, large patches of solid colors broke the huge floor into sections one would expect to find in a kept garden. The birds of spring danced across the field singing their songs of mating while they gathered materials for their nests. Three elk; led by a huge bull, dashed for the safety of the large stand of timber off to the left side of the clearing, as the riders crashed through the last of the underbrush.

A small brook cut through the center of the clearing, almost completely concealed by the cattails lining its edges. To the right, huge granite rock walls formed an impassible barrier, unless one knew the trail that led around to its backside.

E'rik paused at the end of the trail taking in the beauty of the valley. It was here that he felt alive, free from the confines of duty and responsibility. Tom rode up beside him, pointing to the far end of the meadow. A hill marked the end of the field and the riders' destination. Five miles on the other side of the hill lay the village of Hayden, a small farm community with just a hint of city flair. There they would take rest and perhaps even catch a show. Hayden was said to have the prettiest dancing girls in the outer hamlets. Shade passed by the two as they glanced over towards the hill.

"Are we going to look at it or travel over it? I for one am ready for a little break from having this beast between my legs."

"I was just telling E'rik about the girls. I do hope Sonya is still there, she was awful sweet." Toms face turned into a smile as he looked slowly towards the heavens.

"For ten gold, I could be awful sweet." Percy teased as he joined the group.

"It was not the gold. She really liked me, I think." Tom looked down for a moment. "Ah, you're just jealous; I saw the way you were looking at her before I sat down."

"Yes, we were discussing price. We had just settled on three gold when, you offered up your King's ransom. I really should be thankful; you saved me three gold coins." Percy chided.

"Are you guys going to jabber all day? I want to get into town." Al'daLane grumbled as he rode passed them steering his mount out into the meadow.

"I agree." Shade added as he turned his horse to follow Al'daLane.

"Wait for me!" E'rik shouted falling in behind.

The party moved swiftly across the field. At the stream, Sapphire faltered and lowered her nose to the fresh running water.

"Oh come on Sapphire, you just had water at the top of the hill." E'rik pulled up on her reins, but the horse held back. With a little more effort he tugged on her, but the horse it seemed had decided to drink and try as he might, she would not concede. Jasmine and Night Whisper stepped through the tall waterweeds and turned back from the far side as E'rik began taunting his mount.

"Come on, Sapphire, the water on the other side of the hill is much sweeter, Tom even said so. You can drink to your heart's content once we reach Hayden." Again he tugged on the reins but the beast would not budge. Tom pulled alongside the struggling Prince.

"Perhaps the beast is as tired of you as you are of her. Maybe if you dismount and lead her across?"

"I'll not lead her anywhere." E'rik raised his heels in preparation to boot the animal.

"I'd not be doing that if I were you, young Prince!" Shades voice called out.

E'rik paused and looked over at him as he began guiding Night Whisper back across the stream.

"And why not?" E'rik's voice showed his agitation.

"She is not given to force. I hate to side with Sir Tom on anything, but he may have a point this time." Shade warned.

"Yeah! Hey, what?" Tom began to object but Sapphire interrupted by turning away from the stream and stepping gradually back towards the opposite end of the field.

"Whoa!" E'rik pulled back on her reins. Sapphire took three more steps and stopped as if allowing E'rik his control back. The young man pulled hard to the left and she turned back toward the stream, but would go nowhere near it. The group began to chuckle, quietly at first, then building to laughter.

"Mayhap she is afraid of water?" Tom teased. Sapphires ears perked up and her eyes swung round to focus on him. "It was a joke, my sensitive beast." The party roared louder as Tom backed Flaming Crown away from Sapphires glare.

"Perhaps she knows we have company." Shade cut in, bringing the laughter to a quick halt. Gathering at the top of the hill, eight riders now made their presence known. One by one they took up their positions forming a line across the path.

"Who are they?" E'rik asked as Sapphire began bobbing her head gently up and down.

"Don't know and can't say I really like the idea of finding out. Eight to four is not a good match." Tom offered as he pulled Flaming Crown around to face the intruders. The two riders on either end of the line raised their cross bows and began slowly directing their mounts towards the party.

"Eight to five you mean!" E'rik protested.

"Oh no, you're not even going to get involved in this." Tom shot back.

"They're closing in!" Shades voice stayed calm, but urgent.

"I can see that, Shade. What do you think they want?" Tom asked.

The men glanced at each other, then at E'rik.

"How could they know he would be here? They could not have followed us, I would have noticed." Shade protested.

"Magic, perhaps?" Percy offered as he stepped Jasmine over closer to E'rik. Reaching out and mumbling a simple chant, he tapped E'rik's shoulder. "It's not much my Prince, but it should do to get you away from here once the battle begins, you can take three hits before the spell will fail, so make good use of them and keep Sapphire moving, now be off."

"I am not leaving, I can fight, give me a sword!"

The bowmen reached range and pulled up to a stop, raising their weapons.

"We do not have time to argue. Move away E'rik, lest you get us all killed." With that Tom drew his long sword from his shoulder sheath.

"Shade, you take Percy, Al'daLane and I will go left. Be off young Prince!" Tom yanked back on Flaming Crown's reins and turned to rush the attackers. Al'daLane gestured and shouted out a

135

command word. The water behind E'rik burst into a spout, its' spray jetting out into limbs as it reached height. Shade and Percy turned and charged their mounts off towards the right side of the field; E'rik stood and watched, feeling helpless and trapped again as if he were still in the confines of his father's walls.

"Be off, Sapphire!" With his command, Tom sent the animal charging away from the approaching riders.

"The Hells!" Young E'rik cursed as his hands took a tighter grip on the leather reigns.

******

As the Prince was rushed from harm's way, the brothers focused on their dilemma. Six riders still held the high ground above what was to soon become a battlefield. The first two had taken up shooting spots near the center of the meadow. From where they sat they could fire their first volley and dart to safety in the trees on either side of the clearing and reload. The brothers had to close fast and hope that they missed with their first shots.

Tom and Al'daLane made for the bowman on the left side of the field as Tom closed the gap; the bowman fired the bolt, aiming not at Tom, but his mount. Tom watched as the bolt slammed into the heavy leather armor hanging over Flaming Crowns otherwise vulnerable chest.

"WHACK" the impact was solid, but the distance still too great and the leather padding thick, the bolt didn't have the power to penetrate. But it did have the force to cause the animal to stumble. As his huge head went down, Tom leaped from the saddle and did his best to prepare for the short yet rapid ride to the ground. As his feet felt the earth beneath them, his knees bent slightly allowing his body to roll towards the grassy ground; his sword arm drawn in close to his body allowing him to maintain his grip as his feet now raced over his head. With a very firm thump he hit the earth and continued to roll until all the momentum was out of his fall. A bit dizzy, he came to one knee some twenty five yards from his attacker. Shaking his head to clear the ringing, he leapt up and closed in on the stunned man coming up from below the man's right side. He thrust his blade deep into his stomach, forcing the man's body to fall to the other side of his mount. Tom raced around the startled horse and drove the tip of his sword into the gasping man's throat.

"Two more are moving, Tom!" Al'daLane voice shouted from a few yards back. "I'll hang on to Crown."

137

Looking up, Tom could see that, in fact, all six of the remaining riders had begun to move. Two more now rushed towards him, two others were headed towards Percy and Shade. It was the remaining pair that concerned him most. Throwing aside any attempt to hide their purpose, the riders raced for the open space between the two. They were after the Prince.

Across the field they raced towards the bowman, Shade taking a slower approach allowing Percy a good view of his target. As the crossbow leveled on him, he gave the command and fired off his spell. Three tiny red globes of light raced from his fingertips and struck the bowman in an instant. The first slammed into his left kneecap, sending a searing pain shooting up his body, causing him to wrench in pain, firing his bolt high into the air to the mage's right side. As the man lunged forward the second orb hit, landing against his right shoulder quickly burning its way through his thin armor. The impact caused him to reel back as the third orb found its mark. Smoke rose from his forehead as the ball of energy seared into his flesh, his head shot backwards, his lifeless body tumbling to the ground and disappearing in the tall flowers and grass.

Percy noticed the movement of the others from the top of the clearing. He saw right away that the center pair were making for the escape and the Prince. He raised his left hand and the sound of the charging riders brought his attention to his front. The first rider was all but on him as he glanced up, his sword drawn and taking aim at the mage. To save his own life would mean letting the two riders slip past, and then the Prince would be unprotected.

"Toeish!" he commanded. A surge of energy flashed from his left hand striking the lead horse in the front legs. The force of the impact shoved the front half of the animal to the right, causing its legs to buckle and its head to slam down into the grassy ground in front of the second rider. The rear of the animal was thrown violently forward passed its head. Rider and mount crashed to the ground in a jumbled heap.

The second rider had no time to react as his mount's feet were swept from under him, sending it face first into the thick grasses of the open field. The man was thrown like a catapult shot sailing through the air, arms and legs waving as if to give him some control of his flight. The water elemental Al'daLane had called before the fight had begun stood before him like an ominous predator awaiting its catch.

As his body reached the water creature, the element spread out before him, forming a huge wall of water which engulfed him as he passed through it, dragging him to the ground wrapped in an un-breathable blanket of liquid death. The man fought to break free, but all his efforts served only to rob him of his breath, and when he could hold out no longer, he tried in vain to inhale; the water quickly filled his lungs. His body fought to exhale the liquid, and he choked, breathed in and choked again. His sight faded and his nerves began to dance under his skin. His hands tore at his captor, his face frozen in terrified silence, and he fell still.

Percy heard the sound of Night Whisper rushing up behind him as his companion raced around from his right. He looked up just in time to see Shade cut across through the tiny opening between him and the rider bearing down on him. Shade's cloak flew open blocking Percy's view as he cut between them. The rider was startled, but held to his course as this wild man cut between him and his target. He saw the black flowing material of the man's cloak as it billowed up before him. There was a flash of something shiny in the man's hand, it wasn't his sword hand. He could see the man still held it at his right side. With a loud buzzing like bees, there was sudden pressure on his throat and the feeling of warm liquid running down the back of his neck. He thought to raise his hand and strike his target as the rider raced from between them. His hand would not respond and he could feel himself losing his grip on the saddle beneath him; he tried to tighten his legs. The animal raced on, passing his intended mark. The air around him darkened and he could feel his body slipping from the horse.

Percy had tugged hard on Jasmine's reins, trying to cut away from the oncoming charge. He lost sight of the man briefly as his companion cut between them. When Shade got passed them, Percy noticed the rider had veered slightly to his right and was no longer waving his sword. There was a small plume of red feathers sticking out of the man's throat and he was slipping from his mount. He watched as the man darted past him, bouncing like some child's doll in his saddle until he crashed to the ground several yards beyond.

Swinging his head back around, he caught sight of Shade as he swung Night Whisper towards the second assassin. The two animals collided sending both riders hurdling to the ground. Shade was the first to rise; he had let go his sword on impact and now brandished two long daggers he carried in his tall riding boots. The man leapt up, sword in hand and blocked the first strike; the second dagger came up from between them, finding an opening in the man's midsection. The blade sunk deep, and with a twist his assailant finished the job, scrambling his tender insides causing his knees to buckle. He grabbed for Shade, but was met by a firm boot to his bleeding stomach, sending him to the ground.

To his right across the field, Shade heard the clang of clashing swords. He turned, seeing Tom block the rider's first attack, and then stumbling into the second. He could only watch helplessly as his comrade was struck by a firm slash across his open back. The cut caused his hands to go to either side, throwing his sword out into the woods lining the sides of the field where Al'daLane now made for cover. Percy turned Jasmine towards the fight and raced to his brother's aide.

Tom had heard the warning; he turned to meet the advancing riders. The men took a wide berth between them, giving the fighter little choice but to fight. As the first man barreled down on him, Tom caught his swing, blocking it but feeling the pain of the force as it vibrated through his own weapon. The speed at which the man had come at him gave the attack extra momentum, causing Tom's body to be thrown a little off balance as he met the swing.

He spun as the rider raced past him. A mistake, he knew, but the strike had given him little choice. Seeing the first rider pass, he barely heard the second one approach when the burn ripped down his back. He was pushed forward by the force of the blow, his arms flung out to his side and before he could react, the man's horse slammed into him sending them sprawling to the ground. The heavy beast crushed the breath from him as it trampled over his torn body.

Al'daLane saw the first riders attack blocked. As the man raced passed Tom, he focused on the mage. Unarmed and outnumbered, Al'daLane made for cover where he could work his magic. When he heard Tom scream out in pain, he looked over his shoulder to see his comrade fall. Seeing the horseman ride over Tom's body, Al'daLane shouted out the command. From everywhere briars sprung up and shot at the rider like spears. The thorny bushes engulfed the man and yanked him screaming from his horse, dragging him back into the wooded area. The first rider had made his pass; he turned towards the mage but lost him in the thick

143

undergrowth of the small forest. He heard the mage shout, followed by the screams of his comrade. He had not been paid that well, he broke for freedom through the trees. Al'daLane heard the sound of the man's horse growing fainter; he knew the man had had enough; he rushed out to his fallen friend.

* * * * *

Darkness was closing in around Tom; he knew the wound was serious. He could feel himself coughing, though he tried not to. His was hot and cold, his stomach was on fire and his left leg was throbbing. He heard the screams of someone, they seemed far off, and he hoped it was not one of them. Hoof beats shook him for a moment. Was the man returning to finish him? His head pounded, the sound of a thousand trumpets blasted in his ears. He shivered and blackness took him.

"Tom, Tom." A soft female's voice echoed in his ear. *"Tom, you have come to me again so quickly. You must tire of your follies."* A soft radiant light filled his eyes and she began to take shape.

"My lady, where am I? There was a fight…and a scream, I fear…"

"Fear no more Tom; your companions are all safe. But the Prince has fallen into the hands of your enemies. I cannot let you stay. You are needed to guide your friends to free him. I can do little to interfere with the upcoming battle, but know that I am there. Now go back Thomas of Deschutes, tell the others to prepare. A great evil comes to the lands of Coeur D'Alene.

CHAPTER 13

Shade ran across the field behind Percy, racing to Tom. Al'daLane was kneeling over him shouting.

"Tom, Tom can you hear me? Open your eyes." He looked up as Percy pulled back on Jasmine's reins and hoped off the horse. "I don't think he's going to make it!"

"We have to get him back to the castle, they can heal him there."

"He can't ride, Percy. Look at him, that bastard ran over him with his horse and he's bleeding out!"

"I saw what happened but we can't just let him die." Desperately Percy looked to his brother.

"Is he dead?" Shade asked as he approached.

"Might as well be." Al'daLane offered as he rolled Tom over to look at the wound.

"AAAGGGHHH!" Tom cried out, blood erupting from his mouth as his friend lifted his broken body.

"Lay him down, Al'. Tom, Tom can you hear us?" Percy shouted leaning into Toms face.

"Eeevviiiifff...." Tom tried to speak.

"Tom, Tom what is it?" Shade stepped closer.

"E...evil, coming…uh." Tom began coughing up blood as he tried to warn the others.

"Evil. Tom, are you saying Evil?" Percy prodded.

The fighter nodded the best he could; he wished he could find his voice. "Why does the goddess always pick me?" he thought to himself as he lost consciousness again.

"We have to get him to the healer." Percy and Al'daLane quickly gathered limbs from the nearby trees and made a bed for him.

"I have to go after the Prince." Shade threw himself back up on Night Whisper's back and turned him away from the brothers.

"Who were these guys, Shade?

"Falcons, I'm afraid." He tossed the purple sash to Percy as he urged Night Whisper off to find E'rik. "I'll bring him to the castle after night fall. Tell the King, if my suspicions turn out to be wrong."

"Suspicions…?" Percy called out after him.

"'I fear we may have been duped, these men were not up to the task they undertook; I fear the Prince may have run right into the hands of the real kidnappers!" With a shout he kicked Night Whisper and the animal took to a run.

"Do you think he is right; could this have just been a setup to separate us from the prince?" Percy worked as Al'daLane pondered the question.

"They did fall a little too easily; Tom was just got caught in a bad situation. If he had rolled to the side he could have avoided both of their strikes. I fear his concern for E'rik made him stand fast and take the beating. I hope however that our friend is in error. If someone did set us up, it means there are enemies inside the castle walls. And that is never good."

Toms coughing ended the conversation. The men laid their friend on the make-shift bed and started across the field. Each bump caused Tom to cry out, but they knew traveling too slow would kill him as well.

"Where do we take him, the Kingdom is too far and Hayden has no Priest. I keep telling you guys we need a priest to run with us…but no…" Percy began to chastise the group.

"Seriously, you wish to start this now?" His brother cut him off.

"It is just that in times like these, we don't have the luxury of a healer is all, and Tom might die…"

"Don't." Al'daLane drew up short on his mounts reins. "Tom may die…but we don't have a Priest, Percy, and that is just the way it is…so as the others have told you, if you can't handle it…go home.

"HAIL travelers! We are friends. It would appear you are in need of a healer. We offer you ours if you care to have her assistance." A loud clear voice came from the brush off to their left. Neither had seen nor heard riders. They quickly prepared spells and looked around. Thirty yards away through the small trees, a single rider slowly made his way out into the clearing.

"Hold your mount, sir. How is it that we did not hear you and where pray tell are these 'we' you speak of?" Percy held his hands at the ready.

"You were bitchin' too loud to hear anything I would say. We need a Priest…we don't have a Priest…we should get a Priest." The loud boisterous voice took them both by surprise again, as a new rider came at them from the right. Al'daLane turned to face the new threat, his fire spell dancing across his fingertips.

"Oh, and am I supposed to be scared." The rather huge man raised his fingers and began mocking the pair.

"Die we might, but you and yours will know we have fought, so hold your ground big man or suffer." Al'daLane stared in the big man's eyes, watching for any sign he might attack.

"Leroy, knock it off. They need our help not your attitude. I apologize for sneaking up on you good fellows, I am Skythane Paladin of Ishtar, and this is my…"

"Go on say it…" the gruff man taunted, smiling at the more pleasant man. Shaking his head he continued with hesitation.

"…brother. For him, however, I never offer apologies. He can fend for himself, and I assure you if you attack him, I will stay my hand. But for now let me summons our Priestess…Tristan! Quick, he looks worse than we thought." They heard only a swift breeze, and a shadowy figure took form at the edge of the tree line as the Paladin spoke.

"We did not say we wanted your help. How do we know you are not the brigands that attacked us?" Percy held his hands directed towards the one named Skythane.

"I assure you, I never attack in an ambush, for I am a Paladin of Ishtar. I offer you my assistance, sirs, and though you may refuse it, I fear I cannot in good conscious let your friend suffer if I can assist him. So, strike if you must, but again, know I am a Paladin of the King and I assure you, that spell is only going to piss big ugly off…"

With that, he dismounted. Percy turned his eyes towards the huge man still sitting in his saddle. The odd, almost threatening, smile on his face did little to warm Percy's opinion of him.

"Skythane Paladin of Ishtar, Leroy…by the Goddess I thought you were dead!" Shade spoke as he rode up, throwing himself off Night Whisper's back and pulling his gloves off as he embraced the well-dressed man as if they were old friends. Skythane returned the embrace and Leroy simply grunted.

"Finally, someone who appreciates us!" With that, Skythane and Shade turned and shook their heads as the huge form of a man dismounted. "Tristian, get your butt out here and fix this guy." Leroy shouted as he approached the two laughing men.

"Leroy, I must say even in dying you have avoided humility. You are a true Barbarian, my friend." Shade approached the big man throwing his arms to either side showing he held no weapons as he embraced the huge fellow.

"Uh, hmm, hello." Percy and Al'daLane blurted out.

The trio turned to see Percy and Al'daLane standing, spells charged and their jaws hanging wide open. The three men simultaneously burst into laughter.

"Oh you should see your faces…" Leroy pointed at them, wiggling his fingers in jest. "BOO!"

"TOM?" Percy yelled out, his frustration obvious to all.

"Relax, I have your friend, he will be fine. His wounds will take a few days to fully heal, but he will not perish." A soft female voice spun them around; again they had not heard nor noticed her approach. In a fight they realized they would have already been dead, which did not bode well with either of them. They considered themselves seasoned adventures after all. As they watched, the young priestess stood and walked casually past them. Her stature was that of a healer who had seen many a fallen comrade. There was something very uneasy about her presence. But neither of them could put their finger on just what it was as she strolled by, joining the others now chatting and carrying on. Percy was the first to release his spell and rush to Tom.

"Tom, the healer says you're going to be okay, but you need some time to heal from the cut. We need to get you to a town or at least to some shelter." Percy knelt down beside his groaning friend.

"...her hands were freezing cold, like death itself." Tom mumbled as Al'daLane joined his brother.

"Who's hands, Tom?" Al'daLane put his hand on Tom's forehead fearing he had a fever.

"He is probably referring to me; I fear my touch is not that of a fair maiden, I simply impart the blessings of the Goddess. I often forget to warm my hands before saving someone's life…my bad." Her statement was cold and harsh, no apology offered. She now stood looking at them as if affronted. This was the first time either of them really looked at her. There was a shimmer about her very body, her hair hung close to her frame even though there was a breeze moving most everyone else's about them. Her clothing more reflected the Emerald colors, than actually being the rich color. Her breeches and blouse were almost transparent to them and they stared a bit too long for her comfort.

"Have you never seen a female before?" Her voice drew their eyes to her face.

"Just never one they could see through, I'm guessing." The voice of Leroy chimed in.

"What are you?" Percy found himself saying before he could stop.

"I am Tristian O'Keeph, Priestess of Atheria and blessed bearer of Atheria's Redemption, slayer to the undead and the keeper of all that she deemed worthy…" She suddenly stopped and looked over her shoulder.

"…worthy." The huge man stood behind her taunting her and mimicking her words, gesturing with his hands. She turned quickly, causing him to drop his hands and his mimic.

"One day Leroy, the Goddess will bid me to smack you, and I will revel in great delight as you soil yourself."

"Ha ha, ha." The entire group including the priestess took to laughter.

"So, what happened to you my friend?" Skythane brought the band back to the seriousness of the situation.

"Did you find E'rik?" Tom did his best to sit up.

"No, whoever they are, they knew what they were after and they knew how to get him separated from us. I feel the fool here, I of all should have seen the intention. There have been many rumors these past few weeks floating around the Kingdom. One of the caravans coming in for the celebration was attacked and all they took were garments for a performance the theater group was supposed to put on. His majesty felt certain they were planning to move against the Kingdom the night of E'rik's birthday celebration party. I fear now they were perhaps just using that as a ruse to get our guard down. And now I have fallen for a most simple of ploys. Darrin will have my hide." Shade offered, shaking his head as he spoke.

"The scheme seemed quiet elaborate to me, to draw you away from your charge thinking to keep him from harm's way, how could you know they were coming after him. Anyone could have fallen for it." The Priestess offered in condolence.

"Yeah, if they are total idiots. The Prince was with us and I should have insisted he stay with us. Instead I let a few cheap hooligans fool me into sending him off, on his own. Thinking a simple horse could protect him better. No, you are too kind Mistress Tristian." Shade gave a simple bow.

"I still say anyone could have fallen for it. What are the odds he would have wandered out here with you on this day? Perhaps it was a scheme of opportunity and not aimed at you at all." she countered.

"Really Tristian, you're going to debate tactic's…really?" Skythane interrupted.

"Hee hee" Leroy snickered from beside her.

"You guys leave her alone." A harsh female voice jerked Percy and Al'daLane around again. To their surprise a tall slender half-Elf female now stood thirty feet behind them just on the edge of tree line. From her clothing they took her for a mage, from her staff they took her to be a very adept one. She wore a simple cream blouse, the front laced with white silk ribbon. Her tan breeches were laced from the top of her knee-high riding boots to her thigh with the same silk lace. A long flowing robe hung from her shoulders draping down along both sides of her as she stood looking at the pair of young semi-experienced mages. A platinum circlet crowned her long blonde hair, an exquisite gold inlayed, rose shaped ruby center piece finishing it off.

But it was her staff that made her unmistakable… the Black Rose of Zarett. Only one existed and only one person had it…Renna WhiteLace! The huge crystal rose sat atop a six-foot black steel staff. Indeed it was from the black steel the staff took its name. Rumored to allow the wielder a most devastating battery of spells and protections from all but the highest level of attacks, the Black Rose was the most envied of Staves, and Renna was said to have come by it simply by stumbling upon it while fighting alongside…

"By the Gods and Goddesses, are you to tell me this is the fabled motley crew of the 'Fates Favorites'?" Percy mumbled, his words fading as his eyes began scanning the group now assembling before him. The tall human dressed in white clothing would be Skythane Darrow, Paladin of Ishtar, his clothing rumored to never soil. The huge man next to him would be his twin brother, the obnoxious

Leroy Darrow, the hammer-wielding Barbarian. From his belt hung the two massive hammers, Leroy's Boom Stick on his left and hanging on his right, rumored to have come from the Goddess herself, was Ishtar's Messenger. The translucent Priestess would be Atheria's ethereal servant, Tristian O'Keeph, saved from death by her Goddess and presented with Atheria's Redemption, given her to defeat the demon Lord Sol'o'Mon in the battle for Coeur D'Alene. It is rumored that the experience of having the hand of her Goddesses laid upon her, turned one of her eyes a different color. These accounted for would mean that there are still two unaccounted for Kia SilverSheath and Chaz Raboza. Just as he was turning to look for the other two, they rode up.

"No sign of the riders or their quarry I fear, Skythane. Whoever attacked them is long gone." The man spoke as he dropped off his mount. A quiver of arrows strapped to his thigh, another sprouting arrow tips from across his shoulder and the ominous Blessed Elven Bow strung across his chest, Kia SilverSheath.

"I did find residue from a teleport spell on the trail back about a quarter mile. My guess is they set it and then chased their prey back through it. The spell was too long gone for me to track its destination. I am sorry, my friends." The second much younger rider offered as he dismounted, Chaz Raboza.

"You can close your mouth any time, young adventures. We know how it is to be inexperienced and to be surprised." Renna offered as she nodded her head to the two brothers.
"You're...you, but how...why are you here. I heard you were all dead?" Percy muttered out as he looked them over.

"We keep hearing that." The group chanted in unison.

"We had a close call for sure, but Ishtar is a mighty Goddess, and Atheria a gracious Goddess. They felt perhaps there was more we could do for our Fath...homeland. So they intervened on our behalf, as it were." Skythane shrugged.

"She just really likes me. He is a little jealous so he comes up with these stories." Leroy interjected.

"You are a blasphemous fool, Leroy, and one day, you will feel her wrath." Tristan stepped away.

"I take it you two haven't made nice yet?" Shade stood next to Leroy both watching as she walked away.

"Nah, and you know how she can be" Leroy offered as he turned to face Shade. "So what the Hells happened?"

"I do not know my large friend; I do intend to find out, however. I fear there must be a rat in the sewer, and I hate rats. I will take my leave if you can accompany my friends here to safety." Shade turned and remounted Night Whisper. Giving a nod he turned her back to the city.

CHAPTER 14

"Wouldn't want to be in his boots, Dad is going to be pissed." Leroy let out a low snicker as he watched Shade ride away.

"Keep that to yourself," Skythane ordered as he nodded towards the trio now gathering themselves up. Percy assisted Tom onto Flaming Crowns back; he was sore but able to ride. They would not need to hurry for now they were in the company of very well-armed and well-trained companions. Leroy looked to the group.

"So you don't think they know who we are?" he jested.

"I do not believe your King has shared that with everyone in his Kingdom, dear brother."

"What? He's ashamed of us or something?" Leroy grunted as he threw himself on Tond'ra.

"You know that's not it, Leroy. You're just being an ass and you know it." Skythane walked to the edge of the trees and summoned Purefire. He would take the lead and scout the path to Hayden. Word would travel fast about the Prince being abducted and he wanted to be ahead of it when it got there. He was hoping someone's reaction might give him a hint as to the abductors.

"Yeah, yeah, you're the understanding son, remember. I just think it would be better for the realm if his enemies knew he had more than one heir, E'rik might not be in the danger he is in right now. How's that set with your Paly'ness." Leroy could be harsh at times. But Skythane knew he was as concerned for their younger brother as he was.

"We will travel to the town with you; once we have your friend settled, Leroy and I will go after whoever has taken the Prince. Renna, I want you to go see if you can pick up the trace of that spell. We will rejoin you there. Kia, I am going to want you to come along and stand guard for our return. Tristian, you and Chaz will stay with them and escort them back to the city and we will rejoin you there." Skythane turned to the group as he mounted Purefire.

"We will come with you. He was our charge and Tom will recover just fine." Percy objected.

"I was not asking for your input, good mage. I was telling you what is going to happen. I do not have time nor interest to argue with your wounded pride. You will do as I say, and that is the end of it." Skythane turned and rushed ahead.

"Who does he think he is?" Percy quipped as he threw himself up into his saddle.

"He thinks he is one badass Pally, and unless you can think of a real quick way to get him out of that gear he is wearing…trust me…he is." Leroy gave Tond'ra the boot and raced off after his brother.

"Renna, tell Skythane I will be watching if you run into more than you can handle. And be careful my sister, I get a sense, I fear, this is more than a simple kidnapping. There is evil in the air and it is growing." The Priestess turned to the remaining brothers. "Are we ready?"

"I guess we have no choice, but where is your mount?" Percy asked.

"She travels the planes brother; do you not yet understand who they are?" Al'daLane scolded.

"I know who they are supposed to be, but those are mostly rumors…are they not?" He turned to find the woman had vanished.

"I am beginning to think they are not. I'll lead. You follow and watch for any sign Tom needs us to halt." Al'daLane directed.

* * * * *

Skythane pushed Purefire hard, not wishing to leave the wounded behind, yet not wanting too much time to pass allowing the residue of the teleport spell to fade beyond the reach of Renna. Hayden lay just miles to East and with any luck, Renna will be able to trace the spell and have her own portal ready when they returned.

Hayden was a little hamlet, barely reputable as far as Skythane was concerned. He made it his task to avoid it whenever possible. They rode into town and he let Leroy do the bartering. He sat nervously as his bother entered the small inn and quickly returned. He had hoped that his faith in Ishtar would allow him to single out any obvious accomplices, but in a town full of roughens and thieves no one stood out.

"You pay for the room?" he asked as Leroy returned.

"I told them the King had men coming in and they should make sure they are comfortable. They didn't ask for payment." Leroy tossed his large frame up into his saddle and began turning back from whence they came.

"Really?" was all Skythane could bring himself to say.

"You're welcome." Leroy made a wave with his hand as if to offer his bother the lead. Skythane shook his head as he gave Purefire a nudge with his boot. They paused long enough to tell Percy and Al'daLane to announce themselves as the King's men. If they didn't return by the time Tom could travel, they were to head back to the Kingdom. They were out of sight before either of the brothers could offer an objection.

"Do you think they will believe we are the King's men?" Tom mumbled from his stretcher.

"I will assure them if they have question." Tristan appeared next to him floating just above the ground.

"So you really are ethereal then?" Tom looked up at the translucent figure drifting beside him.

"No, you are delirious; it is probably the fever from your wounds. I would save my energy. It could be worse than I thought." She teased.

******

Shade rode hard into the night. He would have to use the thieves' entrance and send word to Darrin so as not to alarm the people. He only hoped he could get in without one of Sulaunna's ever-prying spies spotting him. The last thing he wanted was to be the one telling her the bad news. Darrin would be hard enough. As he approached the walls of the castle, he stashed Night Whisper in an oak stand outside the killing range. With any luck the guards had already taken the sitting watch and his entry would go smoothly. He had made certain he had not been followed. But the guards would need to be placed on high alert once the King was informed.

He snuck in the old drain and crossed into the thieves' quarter. Rushing along the inside wall he made his way to the courtyard. There he found a young errand boy and sent word to Darrin now all he could do was wait. He took a seat inside the Watering Hole, the least respectable tavern in all of Coeur d'Alene. It only remained by the grace of the King's favor to his beloved, once the leader of the thieves' guild. Many say she stole his heart. Shade knew she had found his graces through other avenues. An hour passed before there was any response. Darrin entered dressed in the hooded disguise he had used on many occasions when he and Sulaunna had been courting.

"What is this nonsense Shade? Where is my son?" His voice was controlled but Shade could sense the fright.

"We were duped your majesty, someone went to great lengths to separate us from the Prince. That someone knew of the mount and of our intentions to go out. There are only a few that had such information."

"Give me their names and I shall have them hung by sunrise and my son returned." Darrin's voice grew louder.

"My King, I fear that is not wise. No doubt they knew it would not take long for us to realize their identity. I would be surprised if they remain within the city walls. I will seek them out and we will return young E'rik to you. I know after today this is a hard request, but I ask you trust me." He gave a bow with his head.

"You should not stay long here, I fear they may be watching you and if desperate enough might move against you if they thought you unguarded. I will remain in the city undercover for a night and look into it."

"Shade, you have never failed me. I will trust you until tomorrow evening. Then I will take this into my own hands." With that he stood and made his way out of the tavern, his heart aching at the thought of having to tell his beloved the news.

CHAPTER 15

The wine and emotions finally took their toll on Namsilat as well. Slumber found him, but rest did not. In his dreams he ran the small dirt streets of so many towns they fled in his youth. Elf and human voices alike taunted him as he tried to get away…

"Half-blood, no one wants you…even your dad couldn't live with his creation…mutant…" He tossed and turned, games of the heroes flashed from a simpler time when his half-blood was still easy to conceal, when the other children would play with him.

"I'll be Bonner Ferrie...."

"You're always Bonner...be the demon!" a cruel young voice called out from the edges of his dream...his body shifts, becoming hideous as he ravages the many villages he and his mother had been forced from...

"No, I am Bonner, I am...he...he was my, my father!"

In a sweat Namsilat awakens from his torment...Doro and Ish stand staring at him.

"I told you it was too much for him." The Priest mumbled as he turned to look at Ish.

"He just ate bad fish last night. It was but a dream of food sickness and he is fine. Ah, he awakens. "

"Good morning, Namsilat. How did you sleep?" Ish's smile was a little too brimming for his mood.

"I did not sleep, Ish. I struggled the whole night with foul memories and spiteful revenge. Where am I anyway?" He looked around. Barmaids were huddled by the stage, mumbling and gawking as the two small beings assisted him to his feet.

"Seems you chose to sleep on the floor last eve. We awoke sometime before dawn, but you looked so tormented we dared not roust you. I do hope you can forgive us." Doro lifted him from the floor; human ground was always harder than any dirt he ever chose to sleep on. As he stood, his stomach threatened to leave him; he ran for the exit...outside he threw up all the wine and ale his body could not contain. Dropping to his knees by the horse trough next to the inn, he began washing his face and head with the stagnant waters.

"They have bath houses here, Namsilat, if you needed a morning bath." Hea'fxtrot's voice called out as the tall man approached.

"He had a rough night it seems. The fish did not agree with him," Ish offered. Namsilat could not tell if he jested or if his dreams had not been as disturbing outwardly as they were in his mind.

"The fish was fine; I however found much that was difficult to digest in last evenings unveiling as it were." He let the water drip off him as he stood.

"Darrin feared it might have been too much. Shall we sit and try to get more nourishment back in you? I fear if last night was hard on you, today's revealing may put you to bed rest." The shaman held his hand out towards the inn's doorway, suggesting they return inside.

"Uh-oh …this doesn't sound good." Doro looked at Hea'fxtrot.

"We should get Namsilat out of the morning sun…and the curious ears of the people. No need to disturb them on the eve of such a wondrous occasion…shall we?" He waved his hand towards the door which swung open, as if some unseen person had opened it for them.

"Nice touch." Ish gave a teasing bow as he walked past the tall man. With a slight rise of his right eye brow, Hea'fxtrot teased back.

"You like that? I could perhaps teach it to you if you have the aptitude." The pair began to laugh as they ushered Namsilat back into the darkened inn.

"What's this all about, my fine dark-skinned friend?" Ish sat himself at the nearest table as the four companions reentered the room. He watched as Hea'fxtrot signaled for the maids to close up the shop they had been so busily reopening.

"What, no food or drink this morning?" Doro grumbled as they departed.

"Darrin has asked me to assemble you in private, he did not mention food…but he did mention NO drink." The taller man pulled up a chair and sat next to the Gnome.

"And what of Moyie?" Doro continued as he made his way to the keg hanging out of the wall behind the bar.

"I am here, my stout little fellow. Perhaps wine for me this morning, Namsilat anything for you?" The gentle presence of the Elfin Ranger did little to calm his restless mood.

"No, I think I had just about enough last night. After I hear whatever Darrin has to say this morn, I shall retrieve Lester and be on my way. I have much to consider this day, and I think better from the road, I fear." He turned and started back out the entrance.

"I would ask that you stay, my young friend. Hear an old fool out and then if you still choose to leave I shall see to it that you are fitted with all your needs before you go." Darrin now stood in the doorway, the White glistening Armor of the Planes lighting the whole room as he entered. Ish and Hea'fxtrot began casting up Wards of protection as soon as they spotted him. Doro set the tankard he was drawing from on the bar and offered up a quick prayer. Namsilat's head began to spin. His nerves went into defense mode and the Talon sprung into his hand.

"What is this?" As always, Namsilat just assumed it was about him.

"Relax my young friend; I am afraid that old habits die hard. I have not donned this armor in many a day, and seeing it must have brought concern to my old friends." Darrin offered a bow and gestured for the others to relax.

"I sense that their concern is justified, if not for me, then for you." Namsilat re-sheathed the Talon. "I do not profess to deserve your confidence in matters of the state your Majesty, but it was you who offered me welcome into this sacred circle, so please do not now try to conceal your concerns from me. If you wish to speak in private with your friends…" He looked around at the gathering… "I will see myself out." Namsilat again headed for the door.

"I ask you to stay, for you are as welcome this morning as you were last night. I am troubled as you sense, a gift from your mother I would assume. But I must ask you to think hard on your choice as to what you hear this day. I will not ask that you make a decision in haste, but I must ask that you practice prudence and some deserved faith in my sharing." Darrin looked hard at the young man before him.

"You have my word, your Majesty." Namsilat offered a bow.

"Please Namsilat; I can never expect reverence from any of you gathered here. Rise and hear me as a man, but more so, as a friend." Darrin's knees weakened and Namsilat had to catch him as his body leaned to his left side.

"Your Majesty!" Namsilat called as he grabbed the man's arm.

"Darrin!" The others called out in unison as they rushed to his aide. They helped him to the nearest table as he began to weep.

"By the gods, Darrin, what is it?" Doro starred long at his friend, he had never seen him shed a single tear in all their journeys together.

"It's E'rik." was all he could say. He began to cry openly as the others turned to one another. They could only fear the worst. But the worst was far graver than any of them would guess.

"What happened, did those damn fools get him hurt?" Doro prodded. Darrin simply shook his head and sobbed louder.

"I told those fools not to give him that horse, is he…is he dead?" Ish asked.

"By the Gods, I hope not. My heart could never heal if I have lost another child." Darrin shouted out. "I fear it is the curse and it has come back to reap its revenge on me. They have taken him…" He dropped his head to the table and sobbed.

"Who has taken him and how?" Hea'fxtrot asked.

"I do not know who as of yet, but I fear it only a matter of time before they make their identity known. We foolishly allowed him to go for a ride yesterday with his unskilled friends. They were ambushed and Shade returned to tell me of their folly. They are young and inexperienced, I should have sent guards…I am getting carless." Darrin shook his head.

"We were young and careless once, my friend. We did alright. I can set out for him if there is a trail." Hea'fxtrot offered.

"Shade feels there is a traitor within the walls; he believes they intend to use E'rik to gain my throne, so for now I am fairly certain he is alive. They were ambushed yesterday and young

Thomas was wounded, his companions have taking him to Hayden for assistance. Shade was going to look around the city to see if he spotted anyone that might be involved and then report to me. I fear the vapors of their escape will have long dissolved in the air, my friend."

"Scrying perhaps could reveal their location. We should muster the guards; if they do attempt to enter the city we will be ready my Lord."

As Doro stepped towards the door it sprang open and Shade raced in carrying the unconscious body of the young Prince.

"Quickly clear a table…"

"By Thor, how…?" The Red Priest shouted out as they cleared a space and Shade laid E'rik down.

"No 'twas by the magic of Renna WhiteLace, I believe." Shade announced as he stepped away from the Priest. Doro wasted no time in beginning his prayer. Hea'fxtrot turned to Shade, a startled look on his face.

"How do you come by this assumption, rogue?" his voice bordering between offense and hope.

"They are here. They actually came to our aide after the Prince was taken from us; she and Skythane were going to attempt to track the villains. I would remind you, mage; your Queen is a Rogue." Shade shot back.

"Correct me not; it was your foolishness and ignorance that put the boy in the grasp of these criminals. How dare you bring the name of the Lady into this…be warned." The huge man glared as he offered his threat.

"If you two children are done. My son is hurt, my people in danger and I would warn you, Master Hea'fxtrot, this is my kingdom and the rogue is as much a part of it as are your people. Can we now think of something besides our hurt pride? You can take your squabble up with Renna when, and if, she arrives, my old friend. As for Shade, he is simply the messenger.

"If the Fates have returned, Darrin…" Hea'fxtrot began to retort.

"I believe he knows the curse, old friend." Moyie interjected for the first time in the whole of the chaos. The tall man eased his posture and shook his head in agreement. The entire room took on an even more somber aura. Namsilat finally spoke.

"I don't know the curse. Might someone inform me?" He looked at the group scanning each face just to have it turn to the King. Darrin stood away from Doro as he feverishly worked to revive E'rik.

"I believe that task falls to me, my young friend." Darrin began.

"Many years ago a great darkness fell on this realm. The King, my father as it were, had become so corrupt in his power and lust he abandoned his people. As corruption is like a plague, it soon spread to his Governors and Barons. Everyone became obsessed with wealth and power. My father had an eye for the ladies and soon his court began to use it to gain his favor, offering him the beauties from their villages and hamlets. His bastard offspring threatened the

lineage of Coeur d'Alene. The most corrupt of all his subjects was a

mayor of a small village on the borders of the Elven lands. Na'pal,

Condon was his name. He discovered the growing population of

unlawful children and devised a plan to ensure himself power. He

turned his village into a sort of orphanage for unclaimed offspring of

the errant King. At first it sounded harmless enough. He, the King,

could continue his unfaithful rendezvous and Condon would have his

henchmen pick up the pregnant females and take the children at

birth. It went well for several years..."

"And then?" Namsilat called for more as Darrin took a
breath. The King held up his hand asking patience as he took a seat
next to the table E'rik now lay on as Doro prayed over him.

"And then, as is the way of nature, or according to some, the

Fates, took notice of his follies. Some say it was the answer to the

prayers of his affronted wife. Others say it was the dabbling of

Condon to strike a deal with any deity that would accept his offering,

and some say it was just bound to happen. But the Gods, two

actually, Kyxlene the Goddess of Torture and Qymeus the God of

Justice, took notice. A Priest of Qymeus appeared in the village and

Condon turned the temple over to him and cast out the Priests of Atheria.

The King would make yearly visits to the town and when those stopped, darkness fell over the place. Minor demons would visit and take the offspring offered up by Condon. At first it was the illegitimate children, but then the townspeople were forced to offer their own children. A young man stood up against these demons on one such visit, a farm boy, really, armed only with a pitch fork. Just as it appeared he would perish in his foolishness, two warriors raced to his aide. They saved him but the demons made off with his beloved. Heartbroken and desperate he joined the pair and set out to rescue her…it was a fool's errand."

"It is water so long under the bridge, Darrin." Moyie spoke softly from behind Namsilat.

"It was you, the young farm boy, and illegitimate bastard of the King. And it was you, and my Father who came to his rescue." Namsilat turned facing the ranger.

"Aye, it was them, and they would do it again given the choice, Darrin." Doro looked up from his prayers.

"But if I had not been so cocky, this could all be behind us and E'rik…"

"Will be fine, your majesty. He was simply drugged and the affects would have worn away within a few days without my aide. They, whoever they are, did not intend to kill the boy. Hopefully Skythane and the others have squelched this before it began." Doro walked over to Darrin's side.

"So, that is how your father got involved, and eventually, costing him his life, Namsilat. I offer you what apologies I have." Darrin offered.

"You owe me nothing; I have come to believe it is as Master Doro speaks. He would do it all again, even knowing its outcome. I am glad your son has been returned to you. I will take my leave as it would appear the danger has been ended." He gave a short bow and stepped towards the open door. Moyie followed him out.

"You almost sounded convincing back there Namsilat. Might we speak a bit?" The Elf fell in next to him as he headed towards the keeps gate.

"It is a free city, Moyie, but if you wish to rehash the past and try to make it more pleasant than it is, save your breath. I heard the story, over and over as a child. Just because I now know Bonner was my father doesn't make the tale any less impressive, nor his departure any less painful." Namsilat fell into a brisk walk down the center street of Coeur D'Alene. People had gathered and stood staring towards the Keep.

"He will have to address them soon if he hopes to avoid frightening them." Moyie looked around as they walked.

"Must be tough having to always tell people bad tidings." Namsilat looked around then back towards the gate.

"Yes, being King has never looked that attractive to me. He has handed down many sad tidings over the years. He accepts his responsibilities well however…unlike many I'm afraid." His words brought Namsilat up short.

"What is my responsibility here, Moyie? You were his friend, the foolish attraction of a young boy cost him his life, depriving you, his friend, my mother and me of his life. Does that settle so easy with a true blood such as you?"

"Namsilat, it has nothing to do with my race and we both know it. He was my friend and I hate to offend one so wounded as you…"

"…but?" Namsilat turned to face him.

"But I knew your father better than you or your mother. I fought beside him in many conflicts; he saved my life more than once. If there is anyone that should feel regret for what happened to your father it is me. I could not save him, nor could I stop him from taking the action that saved his men and the lives of thousands of people living in these lands. You received many of your father's traits, but his selflessness must have gotten buried in your human blood."

Namsilat's hand struck the Elf's face before he realized he had swung. Moyie's head twisted to the side and quickly snapped back. "Feel better?" He simply smiled at the angry young man.

"I...I did not mean to strike you, I apologize." He held his arms wide and opened his fists.

"Seems to be an awful lot of that going around here today." Ish's voice broke the tension. "I take it you said something regarding his father or the lack there of...or perhaps spoke of his sensitive human side?"

"I may have covered all the bases." Moyie nodded at the small gnome.

"So is he in or out?"

"From the smack I'm gonna say in. But he still thinks there is some resolution he can find in the mire of his sorrow. At the least, if he is going to waste this gift the Gods have given him, we may as well point it at something." The two men now stood side by side grinning at the confused Namsilat.

"You two wanna fill me in?"

"All in good time. If you wish to leave, your bill at the stable was settled and Clifford's tab with the vendor has been paid. I do hope that you will reconsider and perhaps give this motley crew a chance to clear some of the fog you have buried yourself in. We have all lost someone. Some have lost many. If you do not learn to let it go it will consume you." Ish offered.

"You sound like an Elf Priestess I know, Ish." Namsilat turned to walk away, thinking of Airapal.

"If it would help, I could give you a big ole kiss." He taunted.

"Let him have his pity. If, as we fear, the darkness has returned, it will catch up with him soon enough. Darrin and the others will require your counsel and I should make my way to my people." The pair turned away.

"I thought Skythane and his band had dealt with the crisis." Namsilat turned back to them.

"You think more then you listen. It is a trait I tried hard to beat out of your father. Good bidding to you Namsilat Ferrie. Should the fates bring us together again I hope you have outgrown yourself." Moyie produced Albescence Hope from his back sheath in a flash and offered a salute. He turned and continued on to the Keep. Ish hovered, watching Namsilat struggle with himself.

"What did he mean by that?"

"I learned long ago not to speak for that one; you could ask him if you really cared. He will be with the King and the others. Namsilat, they are not allowed by honor to tell you these things, but I am not honor bound as such.

There is a curse placed on these lands, a great curse and it appears it has come time for its fulfillment. These men must now prepare to meet it. They would really love to allow you a chance to revenge the death of your father, but if you cannot or will not throw in with them, then they will still do it for you. Of course, they are going to attempt to save a few thousand people and a culture, perhaps even the freedom of all living beings at the same time. But they have awaited the return of this evil for a long time. Your return here signaled that return…at least that is what they are hoping.

"Then they are fools." Namsilat spat at him.

"They have been called that before. The last time they ended up defeating the creature that called them that. Fools they may be, Namsilat, but at least they are doing something about their loss." With that the little mage vanished.

"Whatever with you people!" Namsilat yelled at the empty air. People stared as they walked past him. He turned and stomped his way to the stable. "Good day, sir, I believe you have my mount and I was informed my bill was paid." He approached the blacksmith.

"We have several mounts, sir. The festival has brought many travelers into the city I fear." The man looked around the stable offering Namsilat to locate his steed.

"He is the paint there in the back." Namsilat pointed. As he did, two men walked from the stall next to Lester's. Before he even registered who they were in his consciousness, the Talon appeared in his hand. The men saw the flash and dropped the tack and saddles they were carrying and reached for their own weapons. Namsilat closed in and dropped the first man before he could even get the huge maul up to guard. The second came up with his sword and swung, barely missing Namsilat as he ducked back from the first attack. He brought the blade up, catching the man's sword as it passed in front of him, knocking it from his hand. The man jumped away hoping to make good an escape. He turned and ran for a stall, releasing his horse and, slapping it, sent it rushing at Namsilat as he chased after him. The horse reared up, startled by the blade wielding man. His hoof caught Namsilat, sending him staggering back and knocking the Talon from his hand.

The man had climbed up on the wall of the stall hoping to flee as Namsilat fought with his mount. Seeing Namsilat knocked to the ground he had a change of plans, now thinking to extract some payback for all the coin this fool had cost them. He turned and dove towards Namsilat lying prone on the straw floor. As he fell towards his victim he realized too late that the Talon had somehow reappeared in Namsilat's hand. He tried in vain to stop his fall; the tip of the blade pierced the piecemeal chain armor covering his chest as his own weight forced the blade through him, his lifeless body landing on top of Namsilat. With a quick shove Namsilat pushed the man's body off and rolled over and stood.

"HALT!" The guard's voice made Namsilat shake his head. "Drop your weapon and surrender." The stableman had gone to get the guards when the Talon had flashed into Namsilat's hand.

"Guys, there is a good explanation for this I assure you." He slowly turned finding four heavily armed soldiers facing him.

"You will have time to give that testimony to the magistrate after the festival. Surrender your weapon sir, or be relieved of it. How say you?" The lead guard raised his shield, the other three men followed suit.

CHAPTER 16

Skythane and Leroy ran their mounts as fast as they could to reach Renna and Kia in hopes they were not too late for them to track the residue of the spell which had taken their brother. They gave little thought to what might be waiting on the other end of the portal. By the time they arrived Renna had already prepared her own version of the spell, one which came with a backup plan. Unlike her accomplices, her nature was self-preservation. Rushing head long into battle was fine when one was dressed in steal and the protective arms of a Goddess. But when your thickest clothing is fine satin, you think first. Should anyone be waiting or should there be traps, she added a back door to the portal which would bring them back should they be overrun, and lock out any who might pursue them.

"Are you ready, Renna?" Sky asked as he dropped off Purefire's back, drawing up his shield and offering a quick prayer."

"And us, too." Leroy mumbled beside him waving his finger between himself and Renna, as he gazed skyward his fists closing tightly around the grips of his two huge hammers.

"Yes. I have set a contingency on the spell and Kia will keep an eye out for us should we return unable to speak or move. I do hope the Goddess is not busy, Skythane. We have no idea where this leads or what waits on the other side, wherever that might be." She gave the last command and the portal shimmered before them. "After you." She waved her hand towards the gateway.

"Leroy, you get to be the wall Renna, stand behind him and get ready."

"As always." Leroy began bringing his raging blood to boil, hopefully there would be someone or something to direct it at. As Leroy began grunting and growling Sky stepped through.

"Awk-tu'us-Say-paw!" The sound hit Renna's trained ears like a warning bell.

"Dragon Speak!" She began quickly weaving a spell to shield her from the one thing she hadn't expected to be waiting for them, Dragon's Breath, and from the command she knew it was going to be powerful. Skythane heard her warning and the chant following. He knew enough about spells that hers was going to be centered on her...as was her way. He knew also that having heard the complete cast she would be lucky to get hers up before the force of the attack hit.

Leroy could take just about any amount of damage a Dragon could spit, but Skythane was not so hearty. He quickly shifted his strategy to defense and brought his shield up between them and the would-be assailant. The bright blue hue of his blessed shield quickly engulfed the trio, just as the first wave of the spell hit. The crackling freeze surrounded them completely as the frost breath exploded. Ice quickly began to form around them as well.

With the brief reprieve, Skythane looked around, taking in the surroundings. If it was going to be a fight he wanted to know who held high ground. To his dismay he realized they were in an enclosed structure, a room, not the typical location for a Dragons lair. The grunting behind him told him he needed to make a move before the raging Leroy inadvertently made a foolish move and tried to break out of the barrier now protecting them from the onslaught of frigid air blasting them. The ice was beginning to thicken around the walls. If they waited too long they would be frozen solid, not something any of them wished to experience…again.

"Renna, if you're ready I am going to rush through this blizzard and attack." He yelled against the deafening roar of the breath, and then he heard the sound he had hoped to avoid, a faint whisper from behind him.

"Boom." With that Leroy, in his enraged state, stood disregarding the danger and hurled his thundering hammer towards the assumed beast.

"Shit…no…Leroy! Renna cover your…!" Skythane yelled out his warning as the sonic boom released from the hammers impact demolished the small room and despite his own experience with the weapon, Skythane found himself shocked momentarily from the concussion as it reverberated back at the small rescue party.

When Leroy stood to make his attack, his upper body inadvertently cleared the protective edge of his brother's shield and the breath weapon hit him straight on. The force proved too much even for his rage. The cold stung the naked flesh of his face and took his breath away as it crystallized the air in his lungs. The impact, too, was beyond that which he could withstand and his head was knocked back as if struck by the tusk of Nightmare beast head on. The force rang in his ears as his feet left the ground and he flew backwards, slamming into the much smaller Renna as she prepared another spell. Fortunately for her, but not so much for Leroy, the protection magic from her regalia absorbed most of the huge man's weight. The aura swiftly tossed him like a ragdoll, forward and away from her and Skythane, in the direction of the original attack.

Skythane, rattled from the blast of his brother's thunderclap, shook his head, catching a glimpse of the huge mass of his brother as he sailed over him towards the still incoming arctic blast. Instinctively he reached for Leroy's foot and in doing so dropped his shield to the left just enough to allow the edge of his shoulder to come into contact with the spell. The chilling bite caused him to scream out in pain. In a reflexive action he slammed Leroy's body down hard on the frozen floor and brought his shield back up, placing the barrier between him and the blast, but also his Brother. Leroy stood, shook his head and raised his hand, catching the thunder hammer as it raced back to him. Smiling, he spun around lifting it high and slamming it into the ground sending a shockwave into the building's foundation, rushing towards the attacker. There was a loud rumbling; as the far end of what was left of the structure blew away in splinters and the trio found themselves in the heavens. The air began rushing passed their ears as they began their descent.

"Aw shit." was all Leroy said as they plummeted.

"Renna, get us out of here quick." Skythane yelled as they tumbled earthward.

"Working on it." Renna yelled back, her hands waving franticly as they spiraled. "POOF!" She gave a command that stalled their descent. Floating now, they took in the wreckage. Wooden planks and splinters raced by them, shards of ice now melting in the warmth of the sun turned to water as it fell. Crates, bits of furniture, dishes and even bits of cheap armor were in the mess, everything they half expected save one very big item... the Dragon was nowhere to be seen, neither falling nor flying. In itself a relief, yet a grave concern all things considered.

"A trap." Renna simply stated the obvious.

"You're quick, magi girl, I'll give ya that." The now relaxed Leroy offered.

"You know, she could just stop thinking about you and you would go back to falling, wiseass?" Skythane warned.

"Yeah, but then she has to answer to you." Leroy retorted.

"Yes, but he loves me." The mage teased back.

"Me better." Leroy stuck his tongue out like a child making a point.

"You two finished? Renna, I said get us out of here, not keep us hanging around." Skythane shouted.

"Wow, someone's touchy. You need a hug, brother." Leroy held his arms out.

"Renna!" She needed no more prompting. She spun a spell and deposited them on the ground below.

"So, did either of you happen to notice where we were, Pally man?" Leroy jabbed as he brushed off the remains of the fight, though brief and far from debilitating, the hits had left an impression.

"I was too busy looking for a Dragon, sorry. You?" Skythane shouted.

"Yeah I did, but you're not going like it. I spotted the telltale Scales as we came out of the blast. We are at least a hundred miles inside the Badlands border, and if they find us here it will not bode well for Dad." Leroy had a hard time being serious even when he was smashing someone's head in. The Scales were twenty-two hundred feet of jagged rock mountains separating the Coeur d'Alene lands from the Badlands under the rule of King Darrin's most ardent adversary, Lord Dominic Wroughtbringer. Time and time again they had come to the brink of war, only to have Wroughtbringer blink and back off.

"If Wroughtbringer has E'rik, it's not going to bode well for him. Which way to the city?" Skythane asked as he slipped his shield over his back.

"You gonna start a war, brother dear? I would really like to summons my warriors unless you're planning on bringing the Goddess against them. Then I'll just have Renna send me back to warn Dad." Leroy teased.

"Leroy is right, and I know you know it, Skythane. You have no proof and no right to speak for the King in such a serious situation. Your actions as his son, claimed or not, would give Dominic every right to declare war. And the realm would be unprepared for the attack. I suggest we retreat and give the information to his Majesty; he can decide how to proceed." Renna was right, but Skythane Darrow did not retreat.

"We'll return, but Renna can you summon wards to find if E'rik is within range? I would like to at least know if he is here. Once you locate him, we will withdraw."

Renna cast up three eyes of scrying and set them out with E'rik as their target. It didn't take long for them to locate the boy. Screaming out like a beacon E'rik's magical amulet rang back. Gazing through the magic eye Renna could see him shackled and stripped to his loin cloth, his amulet hanging above his head on the pole holding him. Being the suspicious type, Renna could sense another trap, but hers was to report, not assess.

"He is here. I fear, however, that those holding him are not Badlanders. It is well that we do not proceed." She quickly began casting the spell that would take them home again. Skythane grabbed her hands and looked into her eyes.

"Whoa there, Renna. Something you're not telling me?" He held her hand and looked for the telltale signs of deceit. Leroy snickered from behind him. "Renna, tell me what you saw and do us both a favor and save the lying for your suitors."

"He is being held by the Duergar. Skythane, they are expecting someone to come after him, and are preparing a trap. We should go back and warn the King." She jerked her hands free and awaited his response.

"Can you get us there?" Skythane demanded.

"Brother, I hate to side with the one who wears her night clothes in public, but..."

"But what, Leroy? You afraid of a few midgets with hammers?" He was taunting him and Leroy knew it, as did Renna.

"By the Goddess, Skythane, have you forgotten your place here? We cannot attack even the underworld in these lands; after all, they are still subjects of Dominic. He will have every right..."

"I know my place, Renna. If you feel you must abstain I will understand. Be safe in your return and do not tell Father for at least three days. If we have not returned you give him this, he will know what it means and I trust he will do the honorable thing." He reached inside his belt pouch and withdrew a small jewel.

"Brother dear, I am here for whatever, but I have to agree with her. She speaks some reason. If we are going to attack, I think we should at least get a little help, you know, like an army." Leroy grunted.

"I cannot leave him in this peril; I have an oath…obviously that means more to some than others. If you would just send us to his location Renna, we will do our best to secure his freedom. If that means a fight, so be it." He walked back next to his brother as Leroy drew his hammers.

"You heard the man, make with the wavy thing." Leroy pointed at her with Ishtar's Messenger gripped in his right fist.

"Very well, but I shall not wait beyond the three days. If I have not heard I will see to it that your father receives your Heirloom stone. She began her chant and waved her fingers forming the very delicate weave of energy to send her friends to their most certain fate, with just a few minor changes.

CHAPTER 17

"What in hell!" Kia's voice gave Leroy and Skythane a pause. They turned with weapons drawn to face the uncertain voice.

"Shhh." Renna's voice a gentle whisper over Kia's shoulder quickly brought a smile to the gruff face of Leroy; Skythane stood stern and shook his head.

"I knew you couldn't follow simple directions." Skythane half reprimanded her.

"I'm glad you didn't, not that we couldn't handle these short ones." Leroy offered.

"Hey, could someone give me a real quick run-down? I have a feeling I missed something." Kia whispered as he quickly scanned the area for possible shooting locations.

"Yeah, Renna can't follow directions and now it would appear we are all somewhere in the Badlands about to start a war." Skythane scolded.

"I did as you requested, if we perish, your jewel will arrive to your father, with a simple explanation of what we did. I have sent you to where your brother awaits his rescue and the Duergar await your fate."

"That is not what I said…." Skythane started to say.

"Right, I'll find cover. Just tell me when to start shooting." Kia scampered off, taking a position, giving him a clear killing field.

"We do not want to kill anyone if we can avoid it." Skythane whispered after him.

"We're taking prisoners now?" Kia looked at him sideways as if to say 'yeah right'.

"Well unless you have a plan, brother dear, I have a feeling they're not going to just hand him over. You can try a bluff, but the intelligence of the combined Duergar nation is about two, he held up his middle finger in the Paladins face.

"That's one." Skythane responded.

"Exactly." With that, Leroy stood up from behind the small rock outcropping, Renna had generously located for them, looking down into a cavern some sixty feet across reaching up to a hundred feet high. A large fire burned on the cave floor. A single man stood attached to a hitching post, stripped to his under garments.

"I say we move." The big man quickly brought both of his hammers together. There was a slight clang as the steel heads impacted, followed rapidly by the explosion of thunder, Sparks of lightening danced from the heads of each, as his arms bounced back swinging the hammers up over his head.

"So much for that...LEROY!" Skythane stood and rushed for his younger brother in the bottom of the cave. Hoping, oh how he was hoping, Renna was wrong.

Duergar began to stagger from their hiding places, holding their ears, some just walking out dazed from the assault of the thunder on them...many were dead before they even knew they were in trouble. As targets presented themselves, Kia opened fire, arrows soon rained down on the helpless Duergar; they had not counted on the force that came to retrieve their folly. Kia deployed arrow after arrow, ten, twenty, and thirty. Had they lived long enough to question, the creatures would have wondered how an entire army had snuck in on them. Kia SilverSheath was a one man arrow machine.

Those not struck by arrows were soon smitten by the electrical charges Leroy had begun to cast down from his hammer. Duergar struck by the bolts simply exploded. The screams of the dying soon filled the cavern. Skythane rushed to E'rik's limp body hanging from the cross member of the post.

"We are here E'rik. Just relax and we will have you free in no time." Skythane quickly slashed the ropes holding his frail brother, and E'rik fell unconscious into his arms. Tossing him over his shoulders, grabbing his amulet, Skythane turned, taking in the devastation being wrought on the fumbling Duergar.

"Enough!" he yelled out at his companions. "They are defenseless and offer no threat. Cease this senseless killing. We have what we came for. Renna, take us home." With a simple snap of her fingers they stood back at the opening of the portal they had used to enter the first trap.

"Too simple?" Leroy stated as they reappeared.

******

"Too simple indeed. If you will be so kind as to drop your sibling, Skythane, we will relieve you of that burden." The voice was not one any of them expected to hear - Garrett Evileus, Grand Mage and ruler of all that is evil in the world. As the group turned, preparing for a fight, they quickly realized it was time to think. Not Leroy's best asset. Behind Garrett stood his minions, an army of undead.

"I thought we killed this guy already?" Leroy started to walk towards the mage.

"Hold it Leroy, this is not the time. We may have misjudged him last time. Let's not make that mistake again." Sky put his arm out stopping the huge hulk where he stepped.

"Lovely outfit. My dear brother never really did it justice, but I must say you wear it well." The ash-pale image gave a teasing bow to Renna.

"I'll be sure and tell him you said that when he shows up." She hissed back.

"Why you gotta go calling in trouble, one of these ass's are enough don't ya think?" Leroy taunted her.

"Fear not my barbarian friend, my bother sleeps still. I, however, received an invitation to a celebration I must attend. As your father would never, knowingly, allow me to enter his fair city, I decided a private get-together was called for. So we sent for your brother...to ensure his transformation into the ruler he should be. Now if you will release our future King, we shall allow you to escort us to his coronation."

"I am afraid I just can't do that." Skythane gave a nervous snarl with his lip as he spoke. As he did, Renna cast a quick spell sending the limp body of E'rik to safety.

"You are a troublesome lot, aren't you? Very well, I don't need him anyway. Once you get me past the front gate your father's throne will be mine and you shall serve me wine and cheese for eternity. Take them!" With that the mage vanished and the minions fell upon them.

As the horrifying army of creatures faced the small band of heroes, their claws began swiping through the air, grunts and howls filling the silence as they moved to annihilate their foe. Snarling jaws, slime running from their distorted snouts, the stench of un-death assaulting their intended victims long before the first blow was thrown. The outcome seemed inevitable, Leroy stepped forward, not one to wait for the fight.

"Not today." Leroy calmly spoke as his hammer came across, impacting the three ghoulish creatures bearing down on him. As the hammer struck them the resulting thunder clap raced through the mob of undead. The bodies of the three initial attackers dissolved into flying body parts and shreds of rotting flesh. The booming echo slammed into the wall of grey ash zombies like a tidal wave, destroying dozens and sending hundreds flying backwards giving the group fighting room. Kia quickly fell into a flashing arrow volley, unleashing thirty arrows within seconds and falling back to higher ground.

Renna raised the Rose staff high and with both hands bringing it down she commanded "AWAY DEMONS". The magical ring of oscillating energy released by the staff hummed as it spread out through the wave of undead warriors now closing the ground Leroy had just opened. The creatures began exploding, sending them back into the depths of death's hands as it splattered the heroes with disgusting filth of decaying flesh and entrails.

"Did you have to do that?" Skythane turned grinning, as the cleansing properties of his clothing was already shedding the undesired soiling.

"Like you have something to complain about." Leroy grunted as he wiped the slim from his face and spat it out of his mouth.

"Learn to keep your mouth shut." Renna teased.

"Hey guys, if you could focus here, we have incoming!" Kia shouted from his perch as he released several more arrows into the crowd of minor demons. The army of undead continued to grow, the more they killed it seemed the more appeared.

"Why all the dummies? You would think the 'Grandest Evil Wizard' could come up with something a little more…" as Leroy shouted out his wise crack, the ground under the three heroes began to tremble… "I had to ask." He finished as the earth began to quake violently.

"You're an ass Leroy. Remind me I owe you a smack when…" Skythane began his retort as the earth erupted directly in front of the trio, large claws shot up fifteen feet into the air throwing dirt and rock for yards causing Kia to seek refuge.

If we can get out of this, Renna, now would be good." Skythane brought up his shield bringing the aura of Ishtar around them. Kneeling he touched the tip of his holy blade to the dirt, expanding the aura to surround Kia, any undead caught in the field simply turned to dust.

"To Castle Coeur D'Alene." Renna raised her staff high into the air, purple streaks of energy gathered around it, encompassing the inside of Ishtar's holy aura. In a flash they vanished, just as an Ankheg burst free from the ground and slammed down its massive three ton weight into the earth where the group had been standing.

* * * * *

The group reappeared in the center of the great city of Coeur D'Alene, the people scattering as the sudden appearance of four warriors in fighting stance appeared out of nowhere.

Skythane stood sheathing the Blade of Holy Light. He casually turned to Renna. "Indoors, perhaps, next time?" With that Ishtar's faithful follower turned quickly and slammed his fist into his bothers face, knocking the huge man to the ground. "I have waited a long time to do that."

As Leroy picked himself up he simply shook it off and taunted his brother. "Mom's not gonna like that…"

"She said I could; just ask her the next time you're hanging out in the clouds while I'm trying to save everyone's ass." Sky responded as he turned towards the keep. "Renna, did E'rik arrive safely?"

"Yes, my spell went off unmolested." The mage fell in behind him and the four companions made their way to the mighty Keep.

Leroy picked up his pace. Falling in step next to his bother he leaned in and whispered, "You thinking what I'm thinking?"

"Probably and I'm not sure which concerns me more. Thinking like you, or thinking that…"

"…was too easy." The pair spoke in unison.

"Renna, can you make certain we weren't followed? If we were, don't say anything here, wait til we get inside. If my brother is right, I fear we may have played right into his plan, which is really gonna piss me off." Skythane grumbled.

"I shall return shortly. I have a few components I wish to replenish. Give your father my regards and I shall join you at meal." With that she waved her left hand down her frame and vanished, slipping into the ethereal realm to view anyone or anything that might be hiding there. As the images of her comrades took on the hazy blurred look of being out of phase with her, she spotted a blink off to her right. It was as they had feared, but she did not see who or what had followed them.

CHAPTER 18

Tristan felt the tug on here essence. She released the tether holding her to the physical realm and entered the nether, joining with her Goddess.

"My child... there isn't much time." The Goddess' soft spoken voice touched her ears like a mother's kiss on a sleeping child's forehead. *"One comes that will lay waste to all the humans have built. I must ask you once again to be my champion. Many you cherish will perish, but you must cling to your faith. I shall receive them and grant them good passage."*

"I am yours to wield, my Goddess. Simply give me your command and I shall bare it." Tristan responded without question.

"You must go forth this night. Leave these fragile ones to the safety of the living. You alone can view the truth and must carry it's urgency to the King. He must know that this threat, although mortal in its beginnings, carries with it an evil almost as grave as the one he fears. He must not let down his guard or his entire realm will perish and evil will spread like a winter storm across the living. Ishtar's hand will bear strong in this battle, but his alone cannot

stand against this foe. We must join together if the race of human is to survive. War comes. Now look upon your enemy and know fear as it will strike in the hearts of those still clinging to life."

With that the ethereal Priestess of Atheria began to see vast fields in her vision, and a moving forest sprang up. As her vision cleared the trees, it turned to the most hideous of creatures. Wraiths, thousands of them marching like a great army off into the distance, for as far as she could see. The Great white walls of Castle Coeur D'Alene took form ahead of them. The guards stood unaware as the dimensional beasts simply marched through the open gates. Screams flooded her ears, fires erupted behind the mighty walls and in a loud deafening roar the walls fell… Upon the pile of rubble stood a single image…

"Wroughtbringer." With a jerk on her essence she was thrown back in the realm of man.

"Tristan, you there?" Percy's voice caught her by surprise. Turning to him she glared into his eyes, the intense flames of battle glowing deep within her own.

"I must go. You and the others will remain here and you will be safe for a time. When your friend is well enough to travel you must come to the throne immediately. Do you hear me?" She reached out as if to shake the man, her hands passing through his flesh causing him to jump back.

"Whoa, I shall do as you say, but your touch is painful. I'm a friend, you know." The man rubbed his shoulders where the 'Holy Wraith' had passed through him. With a thought she carried herself to the inner sanctum of the Keep of Coeur d'Alene, Doro's holy writ kept even her from entering the castle itself. It is said that none save Thor himself could cross the sanctified barrier.

With her mind she reached out to the Paladin of Ishtar as she entered the Keep. "Skythane, I must see the King, I have terrible news."

******

Not to be outdone, Renna called up an imp to tail the intruder. "Gad, I have need of you, my little wretched one…BE SWIFT!" In a blink came the trembling image of the Imp Gadrash, his essence shimmering as he bowed to his current master. "What took you? I need you to follow that ethereal creature that just crossed the span. Do not get detected and if you do, I shall extend your

216

service here for millennia." Her harsh threats carried weight and the little imp knew it.

"As you wish, master." The small creature disappeared as fast as he had appeared. Her task complete, Renna turned and was about to step from the ethereal plane into the prime when Tristan's essence crossed before her on its way to the Keep. She held her spell up and joined the Priestess at the inner sanctum.

"Tristan, what is it? Where are the others Skythane sent you to guard?" Renna spoke as Tristan willed herself into the prime material plane to await Skythane.

"Renna, I have seen the enemy. It approaches and there is very little time to prepare. We must shield the walls against an ethereal invasion before they arrive." Tristian turned to Renna.

"We ran into him as well. Skythane and Leroy are in preparing Darrin. We also recovered E'rik. Relax sister, he cannot get in here, any more than you can get into the castle. Doro has seen to that." Renna's confidence did little to calm Tristan.

"It is not a single foe we face. There is an army amassing in the nether realm and it will march straight through the gates, unchallenged by the living until it is too late."

"Army…" Renna started to question Tristan but was cut short as the two appeared in the material plane

"Army. What army, Tristan?" Skythane approached the pair for he had heard the Priestess summons. Leroy was close behind him. There was a loud scream in the night sky towards the center of the city.

"That army. They have arrived!" Tristan turned her body, fading with only half of her remaining visible to the physical realm. Her eyes peered towards the human city's walls. Hundreds of wispy Wraiths flew through the vulnerable streets, the helpless screamed as loved ones were slain before their eyes, devoured by the soul stealers. Dozens of the eerie invaders turned and rushed towards the Keep. Knowing her friends could not see the danger, she returned to material form. Raising Atheria's Redemption, she turned and cast up a wall of strength. One by one the beasts began to slam against it. "Arm yourself, Warrior of Ishtar, I cannot hold them all!"

Dogs began to bark, horses whinnied, chickens clucked and scurried throughout town…an explosion rang out in the night and fire erupted along the main gate. The alarm bell finally rang and the militia was rallied. There was no sound of clashing steel, only the all too often shouts of terror as the invisible killers fell upon the living.

"Tristan, I'll hold these. They will need you at the gate if we are to stop an all-out overrun. Renna and Leroy, the two of you had best get back to the King and send Kia out here. Tell him I have some target practice for him…and hurry." With that, Skythane Darrow drew up his shield and Ishtar's Tear, calling forth the little magic he had gotten from Renna. His ever clean cloths transformed into his mighty armor and the blue light of faith surrounded him.

Raising the Tear skyward he prayed out. "Ishtar, grant me your strength in slaying these abominations of life." In a downward swing, the blade glowed white hot, and the powerful bolt of energy slashed across several of the Wraiths as they sought a weak spot in Tristan's shield wall. In eerie screams of destruction they exploded in the sky. He slashed back across in front of him, banishing several more.

******

Gadrash followed the ethereal essence as it raced across the nether, back towards its master. He could feel the tingling as the creature drew near its destination. The glowing portal of the prime material plane shimmered as the small Imp crossed over, getting his first real glimpse of the creature he had been following. The tiny Homonculous, a bat like creature created and controlled by evil mages to do their bidding, crossed back over into the realm of flesh. Its leathery, skeletal wings fluttered as it dropped onto its clawed feet lowering its head and rubbing its greedy little claw-fingers as it approached its master.

They materialized in a humongous cavern, its stone walls rising some hundred feet above the tiny Imp's frame; he could barely see the other side of the huge room. A molten river of lava flowed through its center. Smoke wafted up from the fiery stream. A massive throne sat on its edge. Gadrash held back in the shadows as the creature knelt before the large, dark mass sitting atop the huge stone throne, its back to the Imp. From where he floated, Gadrash could only see the right side of the being that commanded the Homonculous. When the tiny creature had come to rest, it began to squawk out its report.

"Master, it is done. The foolish humans have taken your bait and the one called Skythane has delivered your creation to the human leader. The Wraiths have begun their assault and soon the humans will be busy fighting for their puny lives and you can swoop in and claim your victory. Shall I report to Dominic and have him send in his armies?" The thin slithering tongue of the tiny creature made several quick passes over its entire face as it rubbed its greedy hands together, daring to lookup into its master's face.

"You shall do as I say, not as you presume, creature of design. I fear you have been graced far too long in existence. You have become overbearing and clumsy." With that the huge being shifted on its stone chair.

Gadrash watched as the large scaly snout of a Black Wyrm turned, leering around the edge of the throne. Before he could blink the Wyrm released a slimy ball of gooey acid breath, engulfing him where he stood in the shadows. On the ethereal plane, acid would be no problem, but on the prime material plane it quickly coated his essence and began to melt the leathery flesh from it. Gadrash could do nothing but suffer as the vile liquid dissolved his flesh, draining all his strength just to hold form on this plane, until finally exhausted, his essence abandoned his frame, jettisoning him back to the lower realms from which he hailed. Contingencies put in place

221

long before Renna took possession of the Regalia of Zarett, kicked

in, teleporting the remains of the tiny creature form back to its

current master.

CHAPTER 19

Leroy and Renna passed Lord Doro on their way back to the King's chamber, his mighty maul slung over his shoulder, casting blessings on everyone he passed. Three priests stood outside the King's door, with four mages, protections were everywhere. If one wasn't real careful, it could be disastrous for any mortal or lower demon within fifty feet of the threshold.

"Whoa, guys, really. They need that out there, not in here. If this shit gets this far it will be over. Now, leave these up and go assist the guards." Leroy barked as he and Renna rushed past and entered the chambers where Darrin and Kia were.

"Darrin, we got this. You need to stay here and prepare for the real attack. I have a feeling these things are just to keep us busy while Garrett gets his shit together. We will need you fresh when the sun rises…if it rises" he mumbled.

"Kia, Skythane has requested your presence at the inner wall of the sanctum. Prepare and I shall send you straight away. Be warned, there are Wraiths everywhere out there. Take your best arrows, my friend." Renna began her spell of teleport as Kia drew up a bundle of demon slaying arrows and crouched down.

"Ready when you are." He gave a nod and Renna released her spell, sending him instantly to the battle. Popping out at Skythane's side he quickly released a volley of half a dozen arrows. Wraiths struck by the magical weapons exploded. Puffs of dark ash begin to descend on the pair as they finished up the last of the demons throwing themselves against Tristan's boundary. When the last of these creatures fell, Kia grabbed up his quivers and was going to make his way to the battle in the street. Skythane's hand grabbed his shoulder, pulling him up short.

"Kia, I don't like this. These uglies went down almost without a fight. The guards have been alerted and the defenses are coming up. The Priests will soon make this a fortress against the undead. I think we should hold here and see what's coming. I have a feeling it is not going to be so simple."

"Agreed, these creatures could have simply returned to their friends, instead they just hung there in the air and let themselves be destroyed. Not like any demons I'm used to. What do you think the game is here? Garrett commands many minions that we really don't want to see in the city." Kia looked around surveying the outer walls of the keep.

Somewhere off in the forefront of the city, the low growling moan of the Orc horn began to blow. Installed shortly after the main gate was laid into place, the Orc horn is the city's main warning system for the vile beasts. Rapid reproduction and a thirst for power, coupled with a hate for humans…Orcs can be overwhelming to say the least.

"Orcs…really?" Skythane sarcastically turned to his friend. "This may just be the beginning of a very long battle. Let's mount up and head for the main gate. If he has brought Orcs, surely there will be Trolls and I hate Trolls! I will take command of the main garrison and plan a strategy once I have a good assessment of the force. Your talents will be needed on the walls if we are to keep them from crawling over." The men turned and rushed to the stables.

CHAPTER 20

At the main courtyard of the city, Tristan stood smashing wispy demons as they charged into the gates while the human guards fought to get the doors shut. The city guards had been on high alert for the festival, but Darrin had chosen not to scare the folk by announcing E'rik's abduction. He had failed to post extra priest-watchers or mages at the towers. This was causing undue...'in her mind'...struggle.

"BE GONE DEMONS, by the hand of Atheria I smite you back to the dungeons of hell." In one final two-handed grasp on her flail, she swung it high and slammed it to the ground, sending an energy wave of light through the wall of Wraiths as they flooded through the shrinking opening as the gate crashed together, the sound reverberating throughout the courtyard. A momentary shout of success rose and was quickly shot down as the shadowy figures raced over the tops of the walls grabbing men and dragging them high into the sky and simply dropping them screaming to their deaths.

"Blessed Atheria, give me strength for this battle." Tristan raised her essence into the tower and began casting out the Wraiths as they formed a tidal wave against the wall and flooded their way over the top. Her small, glowing essence, like a beacon of hope, stood beneath the huge surge as it cleared the sixty foot outer walls of the city. As the wave broke and fell upon her, the tiny speck of light vanished beneath it. The silence was deafening as the assembling armies of the King fell witness to the overwhelming power of the demons. For an instant, all stood watching, despair began to fill them. There was a sudden flash of blinding light, and a groundswell imploded from its center. Like a giant vacuum, a swirling vortex of Wraiths were being sucked towards it…their wails filled the air.

"FEEL THE POWER of the GODDESSES, all Demons!" Tristan stood holding her flail high above her head; denizens by the hundreds fought to escape its pull, but were sucked in, howling as they vanished. Somewhere near the base of the wall, the creatures broke off their attack and raced away from the Keep. They fell into a huge cloud of evil, circling around the outside the walls of the city.

"Less pomp, more pop, young one." The voice of Doro caught her by surprise.

"A neat trick for any, but for a Dwarf…impressive." She wrote it off as being so focused on her Goddess.

"If I were an errand boy with a message of death, my dear, we wouldn't be exchanging niceties. You must focus. I would hate to lose such an asset so soon in the battle, tends to affect morale." The old Dwarf grunted as he raised his mighty maul into the sky next to her.

"Always the funny man, Lord Doro I was beginning to think Atheria was going to have to take over security here in Coeur d'Alene. Where have you been? The fight's almost over" she teased back.

"Huh. They seek to surround the city child; a siege is not a good thing. What say you and the Goddess do a little joint communion?" The rugged Dwarf held out his left hand to the shimmering Priestess.

"We are in agreement with you, my stout little friend." Tristan's touch to the unreceptive can kill outright, but even to the accepting it can be painful. As their hands joined, the Priest of Thor felt the surge of energy rush through his body, his natural defense kicking up, bolstering him against the chilling effects. With a shiver he tightened his grip. Tristan smiled a sinister grin.

"Remind me to never, ever snuggle with you, sweetheart." Doro closed his eyes, clearing his thoughts to receive the gift Thor would be bestowing on him. Likewise Tristan breathed in the essence of Atheria as the pair raised their holy weapons into the sky. Bolts of heavenly energy flashed in the night sky, striking the weapons in two large golden arcs. Smaller bolts rained down on the circling demons, slashing large openings in their forming circle. The bolts danced down the arms of the heroes, soon encompassing their bodies.

"COVER YER EYES, PEOPLE!" Doro called out. The men around and below diverted their eyes just as the explosion went off.

"KAWOOSH!" The wave started at the pair, mushrooming out and quickly spreading throughout the kingdom. As the cloud of energy struck the wall of Wraiths, they began erupting into puffs of dark smoke settling to the ground. Those that could, quickly retreated away from the aura, but to the disappointment of the two priests, continued to attempt to encircle the kingdom. Now and again

229

one would get too close to the ring of power and be destroyed. The two would need to stand guard here until some other strategy could be invoked. The siege they had hoped to prevent was on, but they had bought the settlement room to breathe…for now.

CHAPTER 21

In the cell of the city jail, Namsilat heard the commotion begin. At first he thought it part of the festivities…but with the loud explosions and the edge of terror that took to the voices, he knew this was not good. He figured if it got too bad, surely someone would come looking for him, surely? He had just gotten comfortable when the Wraiths assaulted the outer wall of the Keep. The first creature entered through the simple stone wall of his cell, another man would have been easy prey. The Talon flashed into his hand and with a slash he cut through its essence destroying the creature. The next thirty minutes would be constant fighting, his arm grew tired and he began to wonder if perhaps his quick reaction in the stable was not his best doing. Three Wraiths appeared in his small cell and surrounded him.

"By the Gods, does this get any worse?" He hated himself the second he heard his voice say it. The ground beneath him began to shake violently, tossing him to the dusty floor of his cell. The creatures fell on him, and he swung wildly, hoping to stay at least one touch…it was gonna hurt, but three could prove deadly. As his arm swung through the air the three demons popped, sprinkling him in dust. He inhaled the foul residue and began choking and spitting. He didn't know a lot about demons, and he hoped he hadn't just become one. Choking, he stood and began dusting himself off.

"Guards, by all that is righteous, get me out of here, I can't die like this...GAURDS!" There was no answer, and to his dismay there was nothing but silence. "Great, they left me here, the cowards." He could not see the bodies of the two guards that had been watching him and the other prisoners, nor the lifeless forms in the other cells.

Suddenly, there was the sound of crashing metal as if someone had dropped a weapon or knocked over a shield.

"Hello, is someone there? I need to get out there and help the King. You have to open this cage door." Namsilat listened for a response or even chatter. The room remained silent and then he heard the rough sound of a foot dragging across the dirt floor.

"Look, you are going to have to move a little faster if we are going...whoa, where the Hells did you come from?" Namsilat had been leaning on the bars of his cell as the grotesque figure of the dismembered guard slowly moved into his view.

232

"Now this has got to be the worst situation I have ever been in. Come on ugly, step up here and I'll put us both out of your misery." When the undead creature reached the bars it slammed itself against it several times before Namsilat ran the Talon through its head and ended its existence. Pulling the blade back through the bars he watched as it fell and the second guard made a slow dash at him. Namsilat stepped back then hacked the beasts head off, the ringing of the keys hitting the floor lifted his heart…he was free.

CHAPTER 22

Skythane began barking orders as soon as he and Kia entered the guardhouse stables.

"To your feet, Cavaliers! Board your horses. You there, Priest, we will need your prayers and blessings, the undead attack the city and we go to meet them."

Kia busied himself gathering his and Skythane's mounts and getting them dressed. Skythane spoke to his small band. He had hoped for the full garrison, but many had been released for the upcoming festival and the King had not seen it prudent to recall them…yet. He counted twelve. Not much, but he had worked with less. Mounted, trained warriors were effective against the slow moving undead. Tristan and Doro had the Wraiths at bay; now it was time for mop up…at least he kept telling himself that.

"I won't waste time we don't have here. There is a slow moving but deadly force just outside our gates. We are to be the first wave of offense the King is sending. Ride hard, strike fast and reset…you can retreat when you see me turn. Mount up!" With that he tossed his leg up over Purefire, Kia mounting up next to him as the priest finished his blessing and prayer and opened the stable doors. The armored mounts rolled out in pairs behind Skythane and Kia.

"Your father sure knows how to throw a party." Kia laughed as they spurred their horses into a run. Frightened citizens scrambled out of their way as they barreled down on the main square.

"Skythane Darrow and riders coming out, OPEN THE GATE!" Skythane gave Purefire a nudge and she took off, quickly pulling away from the group. Kia tucked tightly at his side.

As the huge gates swung open, the dry dirt, semi-circle known as the killing zone lay before them. Two hundred yards of earth had been cleared and kept that way since the construction of the Castle Coeur D'Alene. Designed to keep large groups of would-be enemies from creeping too close, it served for carnival grounds during the seasonal festivals and grand celebrations. Many carts and tents still stood, but most had been destroyed in the initial attack. Bodies of the innocent lay strewn before the riders as they charged.

Two hundred and fifty yards out, large oaks, some eighty feet high, had been left to mark the entrance barrier. Armies advancing past these trees without invitation or permissions acquired, were considered hostile and the tower Ballista would not hesitate to open fire on them with their massive three-foot shafted arrows, and alarms would be raised. It was an ideal set-up for the protection of the city, but also an excellent location to hide an ambush.

Clearing the gates, Kia opened fire, his demon killing arrows striking several targets as Skythane closed in on the huge pack methodically moving towards the city walls. "I hate archers, those don't count you know." He yelled as Kia reloaded for a second volley.

"Ha," was all he said as he cut down the front wave of ghoulish souls, dropping them just as Skythane closed on them. Undeterred, the Paladin pushed his mount straight into the crowd and began slashing.

"Don't poke me with one of those things." He called out as Kia released a third volley, sending arrows just over Skythane and weakening the rotting flesh wall to clear a path. They had done this sort of fighting before; he knew Skythane wanted a swath through the middle to separate them into columns so the Cavaliers could run them down in quick effective passes. He dare not lose too many of his father's best men on such a weak foe.

Kia pulled up a few feet from the front row of undead as Skythane and the rest pushed through the center. He nudged Target, having him slowly begin walking backwards just out of reach of the lead zombies. From here he would simply fire at will, slaying the slow un-living as they reached for the animal, driven by food lust. Skythane and the Cavaliers broke through the back of the army. Turning, he pushed his mount back into the pack on the right, leaving the left side for Kia.

"Coming back up the right…guide your arrows." As he spoke the man closing on his side yelled out and dropped from his mount. Skythane was too focused on the task at hand to look back to see what had got the man. Two more riders fought their way up next to him, they began yelling…

"Archers in the trees!" As they hacked at the undead and struggled to keep close to the Paladin, they each in turn pointed their weapons off to the huge oaken forest that circled the killing zone outside the walls of Coeur d'Alene. Another volley ripped through the mix, striking several of the undead with no affect, but dropping the horse to Skythane's left, sending the mount and the rider into the mass of undead. The man's screams chased after them as they fought through the crowd, finally breaking out the other end. They had slain dozens, but the line seemed untouched as they turned to the left circling around behind Kia as his mount backed away from the approaching army.

"I hate to say it, but I think someone else has brought archers, and these uglies are either breeding or springing from nowhere. We may..." he paused as he ducked an arrow whizzing between them "...wanna rethink this strategy?" He released several arrows out towards the oak stand.

"Agreed. Men return to the city, we fight again." Skythane dropped from Purefire, kneeling, raising the blade and shield before him he offered a prayer.

"Ishtar, grant me your power, drive these undead to their realm." With the completion he stood holding his weapon high into the air. A ray of streaming blue light sprang from its tip. Like a hot knife to butter, he drew the beam down into the advancing beings burning through them as he slowly waved it back and forth. As the beam struck, bodies would ignite and burn to the ground. Suddenly there was no more undead standing.

Kia paused and was going to offer his congratulations. As he turned to Skythane, a single arrow found its mark, dropping the Paladin of Ishtar where he stood.

"SKY!" Kia leapt from Target and rushed to his fallen comrade. The remaining Cavaliers quickly circled around him as he lifted Skythane's limp body onto Target, and Purefire fell in behind them as they raced for the walls, the Cavaliers covering their flank. The arrow had struck at the top of his collar bone, directly under Skythane's helmet and was dangerously close to his heart; Kia could see blood pump out with each heartbeat as he drove Target harder to save his friend.

"Wounded coming in! Open the gates...get a Priest!" He yelled, not slowing for an instant. It appeared he would run head long into the slowly parting doors. "Come on faster, faster; put your heart in it." Not one for prayers of his own, Kia began calling out for assistance in his mind. His voice took on urgency as he reached the point of no return; the gates were barely open enough for a man to walk through, let alone a fully barded mount and two riders.

"OPEN THE DAMN DOORS; IT'S THE KINGS SON FOR THE LOVE OF THE GODS!" Kia knew as soon as he spoke it that his fears had him gripped, and the realty of losing his lifelong friend hit him. "Don't you go dying on me, you hear me. This battle just started, and someone's gotta keep an eye on Leroy." He spoke out loud as he squeezed through the small opening. Arrows began striking the wooden planks, some whizzing past his head as he charged on to the center of the Bailey. "Priest, Priest, where is the fucking Priest I called for?"

"I am here." A young Priest appeared beside him. They quickly lowered the injured Skythane to the ground, and the remaining riders gathered around them, several taking arrows as the guards fought frantically to reclose the huge gates.

"Damn you, leave us be. Let us care for our wounded!" Kia turned cussing at the volley of arrows being launched at and through the gates. As the huge gates were slammed shut, a dust cloud rolled up covering the group now looking upon their fallen comrade.

"We must get him to the safety of the castle. I fear there is nothing I can do for him." The young Priest shook his head as he looked down at the fallen Paladin. Then the Priest's voice crackled, and took on a long hissing sound. Not taking Kia by surprise, he had heard these tones before.

He felt his hand clasp one of his demon-slaying arrows as he stepped away from the image kneeling over Skythane. Stepping back, he quickly notched the arrow, drawing back on his bow; he pointed it at the shimmering essence. The image raised its head slowly, beginning to take a distorted appearance as their eyes met. Without hesitation he released his arrow striking the creature true, just as it began transforming before his eyes.

"Doppelgangers to arms, to arms!" Kia screamed out and the demon perished as its life was drained by the arrow's magic. Suddenly men and women alike began to screech and howl as dimensional demons burst from their bodies, attacking every human around them. Kia began dragging Skythane's limp body towards the guards' room at the base of the wall tower. Several of the Cavilers circled him, doing their best to escort him to safety. Tossing the unconscious Skythane in, Kia turned and fired several shots at the approaching shifters before slamming the door and listening helplessly to the screams of the dying just outside. Two guards ran down the stairs from the wall, grabbing Skythane at Kia's orders and

241

rushing along the passage towards the safety of the castle. Kia raced up the stairs taking his place next to Tristan and Doro as they held the Wraiths at bay.

"The foul creatures have somehow gotten inside the walls. I fear you must let the Wraiths be and turn the blessing inside to save the helpless." With that he began casting volleys of arrows against the ever growing cloud of evil swirling around the outer boundaries of the killing zone. For every one he killed, it seemed another hundred appeared to take its place.

Then, without reason, the dark cloud simply vanished. Standing in its place, ten thousand Orc warriors now surrounded the Castle Coeur D'Alene. Tristan and Doro slowly lowered their hands.

"By Thor's grace…Orcs!" Doro's statement took Kia by surprise for a moment. Doro turned his attention to the inside of the city walls, shape shifters still running rampant. Raising the mighty hammer of Thor above his head, he leapt off the wall, soaring the sixty feet to the ground below. With great force he drove the maul into the ground and the reverberating ring of pure energy swept through the city streets exploding, forcing the shifters into their true form, making them easier to fight for the guards inside, leaving a

small crater around the red-suited man of Thor.

CHAPTER 23

Namsilat reached through the rusty bars and grabbed the key ring off the dead man's belt and let himself out of the cell. The ground beneath him continued to shake and he feared the ceiling would collapse any second. Checking the other cells as he made his way towards the doors his fears were confirmed, instead of men standing at the ready to be released each cell contained the remnants of humans filled with the evil of the un-death. "Sorry chaps, but I don't think we will need your service. I'll send someone back to take care of you as soon as possible."

Turning to the door he was suddenly thrown back across the dank dungeon, the floor exploding when two huge claws sprang up lashing at the air. An Ankheg's huge mandibles began pushing up more of the floor in its fight to break free.

"Where did you come from?" The Talon still clutched in his hand, he rushed in, hoping to strike the beast down or at least discourage its coming any further out.

"Time to die, beast" he shouted. In a hard downward swing he lopped off one of the creature's foreclaws causing it to screech out and spit at him. Thick black goo splattered the wall around him, but the creature had missed its target. Without waiting for it to gets its bearings, Namsilat thrust his blade into the top of the beasts head, penetrating its thick skull and sending the monster into convulsions as its life drained out. When it fell limp, he withdrew the Talon, jumped over the huge insectoid and ran for the doorway. To his dismay, the door remained bolted from the outside.

"I really must study magic, if I survive this day." He mumbled out loud as he looked around the dark prison. A vent, just barely large enough for him, sat half way up the far wall behind a barred window. It would have to do. Climbing back over the dead Ankheg, he rushed towards the hopeful exit. The old bars were rusted and only took a couple of strikes from the magical blade they gave way. Years of soot and grime clung to the tight crawl space. With every inch forward he cursed his luck. "I thought Dragon lairs were disgusting. They have nothing on this."

Thirty feet in, fate rewarded his ungratefulness by giving him a two way intersection. The passage to the left went up; making the journey more difficult and he assumed it the direction he needed to go. "Of course, and with any luck, it gets smaller just as I reach the end." He mumbled as he made the turn upward and fought for every foot he advanced. Forty feet further he began to smell fresher air. Excitement gripped him and he rushed…one should never rush when crawling around inside a castle's walls.

Just as he caught himself he heard a slight click, warning of upcoming danger. "Oh now what?" He froze, a little trick he had learned from Shade while traveling with the brothers.

"If you hear the trap, freeze or fly. Chances are it was the arming of the trap you heard and if you can get away you might at least reduce the amount of damage you receive. If you can't fly and the trap doesn't blow up on you, you may be able to disarm it if you don't lose your senses and try to step away, but instead use your body to locate the mechanism, which is half the battle."

"And then what do you do?" Namsilat had asked.

"Ah, that is where your training comes in." Shade had so calmly replied.

It was this training that Namsilat lacked. Breathing in, he tried to slow his heart rate and concentrate. He became aware of a pressure under his left elbow, looking down as best he could he saw a small mound pushing against his arm. Gently he slid the tip of the

246

Talon between his elbow and what he assumed to be the trigger. While he held the weapon with his arm, he slowly pulled his body over the pressure plate, doing his best not to release it as he did. Once he cleared the gadget, with all but his left foot, he carefully lifted it off the handle of the weapon.

Nothing happened and he praised himself, not thinking the trap may have simply malfunctioned over the years it had lay in wait. Leaving the weapon, he continued towards the end of the passage, cool air now blew in his face. Sensing freedom, he dashed on. Coming to a corner in the small passage he saw a glimmer of light just a few feet ahead of him, and as he had feared the passage shrunk to only a foot in diameter.

"Fates, if you could just give me a break here." He tossed up his prayer as he pushed his face into the small portal and glanced in. "Oh, this is not good at all." Glancing through the small opening, Namsilat could not believe what he had gotten himself into. The King's Vault sparkled up at him. Looking up as best he could, he simply spoke his objection.

"Really…?"

He had come too far to turn back, yet he knew it very likely

that getting into the King's vault would bear dire consequences; he

would have to risk it. He knew he needed to get out of here and help

if he could, but feared at this rate he may get there too late.

"Atheria, if you're listening and you have any compassion

for fools such as me; could you grant me just a little assistance

here?" He looked back into the vault room. Invisible lights lit the

entire chamber. Vast amounts of gold and gems reflecting their

brightness, armor of various makes lined shelves and stood on

dummies to hold their form. Weapons stood tall in various racks and

lay on tables, jewel-handled daggers, carved Ivory, ornate items

Namsilat presumed held many powers he did not wish to be on the

receiving end of. His eyes fell on two full-sized warriors standing

guard at the door, crystalline statues perfect in every detail and

Namsilat assumed just waiting for his or any unwanted entry.

"So, is that a no?" As his remark left his lips, the door on the

far side of the room opened. He stared out as Darrin entered

followed closely by a younger man. As they entered, the King

walked slowly across the room to a large volume resting a pedestal

in the very center of the room.

"We must open a link to the Elves, son. They may be our only hope if we are to break this siege and stand any chance of fighting these creatures back from our doors." As he spoke, the younger man, Namsilat now assumed to be E'rik, slid a tiny dagger from his belt and crept up on the King.

"We can't have that…the masssster would be upssssset." In a quick strike the attacker thrust his dagger into the vulnerable edge of the Darrin's underarm and the King fell to the floor gasping for air. "Doesss it hurt, human? The vipersss poison will take it's time to snuff out your life. In the meantime I sssshall asssssume command of your throne and make peace with the massster. Your foolisssh healers will assssume the stressss of war wasss too much for your old heart."

With that the man turned and walked calmly to the door way. "Guards, Guards. Quick get the healers, the King has fallen!" With that he turned and smiled at Darrin lying on the floor, gripping his chest against the white steel of his armor.

Namsilat held his breath and tongue; he would do little good letting the man know of his witnessing his act. Ducking his head back from the portal, he felt a stone under his right hand wiggle as he slid back into the darkness.

"Now what's this?" he mused in silence. He remained quiet until he was certain that the guards had left with Darrin and the traitor before he began his investigating. Peering down, he made sure the coast was clear. For some reason the vault door had been left open. Allowing the traitor to return without the King's assistance he reasoned.

He began fidgeting with the loose stone. Growing more frustrated seeing he could not work it free, he slammed his fist down hard. The stone recessed into the others around it and Namsilat felt the small tunnel begin to shift and move away from under him. He tried at first to hang on, and then fell several times as a staircase took shape beneath him and the wall opened up into the vault. All that was the wealth of Coeur D'Alene lay before him. Distracted, he failed to notice the movement of the first Crystal Knight. But the second one got his full attention.

CHAPTER 24

News of Darrin's sudden illness traveled through the castle grounds quickly. It reached Doro as he walked through the city, leaving a slew of shape shifters in his wake.

"Master Doro…the King, he has fallen. You are summonsed by the Prince and Queen!" the young messenger panted out his message.

"What do you mean he has fallen?" The staunch old Priest fell in behind the youth and they made their way to the fallen King. "Sulaunna, what has happened?" Doro asked as he offered up a prayer for guidance, rushing to Darrin's side. The young Queen stood holding the hand of her fallen companion. Usually dressed more casually around the castle, she had donned an evening gown in anticipation of a night with her betrothed. Her raven hair pulled back, braided with baby roses, her emerald green gown flowing down off her soft shoulders. The hem of the gown spread out around her feet as she turned to Doro.

251

"They were in the vault…Darrin was to summons the Elves, but he collapsed. E'rik says he was holding his chest. Doro, his people cannot afford to lose their King right now. You must bring him back. Do you hear me?" Sulaunna screamed at him as he began to inspect the fallen King.

"I will do what I can my lady, but it is the Gods that shall decide if we need him worse than they desire him, not I." Doro gave a glance at E'rik, then back to Sulaunna.

"Of course, Mother, let us leave Lord Doro to his task. The people will need to see one of its rulers, and for now you are all they have. We can do little more for father and he would want you to stay strong." The young man led the distraught Queen from the chamber. Two guards fell in behind them as they walked down the long corridor towards the receiving room. One of the guards ran around and quickly opened the lined glass doors. The would-be young Prince looked up and down the long corridor. Seeing no one, he gave the human female a push, knocking her to the ground.

"You will best sssserve your people here. The Massster doesssss not need you interfering now that everything isssss in place." Sulaunna lay on the floor confused, turning to face her attacker.

252

"E'rik, what-what is this?"

"Your precioussss E'rik is not here, and if you try anything the Massster will feed him to the Banelar, hideoussss creaturesss they are, always hungry and fond of human flesssh." The form stood menacingly over the woman.

"Who are you, what have you done to my husband?" As she spoke, Sulaunna rolled towards the creature she now knew was not her son, let alone human. Coming up at his feet she brought her knee up into his groin, hoping it would have an effect. The beast exhaled in a gasp as her knee found the soft pliable flesh of its mid-section. Bending it as she had hoped, without hesitation she drew her dagger from her garter and placed the blade to its throat yanking the creature back by the shoulders as she moved behind him. Holding him between her and the guards that had accompanied them, assuming they were with him.

"I'll not stand by as your Master, or any other, takes over my husband's lands, and as for my son, his death would bring suffering on your Master's people greater than any fancied illusion he has of power, I assure you. Now what have you done to my husband, creature?" She pulled the blade into the tender flesh, the cold, slimy sensation made her skin crawl.

"Do not think it will be that easy human...sssuffering isss our pleasure." With that the beast tried to pull free. In one swift motion, Sulaunna's blade sliced through the thin skin covering the creature's form and severed its head completely...not what she expected.

Stunned, she was not prepared when the two guards made their move. The first one's hand smashed into her face, blacking out the room momentarily. A bright flash of light blinded her as her head was slammed back from the force of the strike, blood shooting from her split lip. Fighting off unconsciousness, she tightened her grip on her weapon. Her fighting skills kicked in and she rolled with the remainder of the blow. Landing across the room she came to her feet.

"So you would strike a lady? Then this shall be a fair fight."

She tucked the edge of the blade in along the length of her forearm. Pulling a small container of thief's ink from her sleeve, she tossed the black powder into the approaching man's eyes. As his hands instinctively came up to his face, she ducked under him, bringing her hand across his midsection laying his stomach open and dropping him from being any real threat.

The second guard had moved in and she used the first man's body as a shield, twirling around him as he fell forward, shoving him into the second man as he approached. The man staggered. Seizing on his loss of balance, Sulaunna spun her dagger around in her palm, bringing it up and stabbing him as he stumbled. Her blade caught him in a glancing blow across his right shoulder, laying the flesh open, but only serving to piss him off. In reaction, his left hand came across, connecting with the ribs on her exposed right side.

Air exploded from her lungs and she felt her knees buckle. Her dagger flew from her hand, clanking across the marble floor. Her left side hit first, her face catching the corner of a small table as she fell gasping. Her vision blurred and she feared she was done for. Shaking her head violently to regain her senses she heard the heavy foot falls in slow motion as her foe closed in for the kill.

She felt his large hands close around her neck from behind. His fingers tightened as he shook her, choking the life from her. Through fighting instinct, she began reaching out around her, hoping to find anything she could use to break his grip. Her fingers felt the cool steel of her dagger, and she fought franticly to grab the weapon. She closed her finger around the razor sharp blade. In desperation she ignored the pain and thrust her hand holding the blade into the face of her attacker, breaking his grip. He screamed and staggered back away from her. Not wasting any time she took the weapon in her left hand and rushed him, shoving the blade into his throat forcing him back with all her might, holding him against the wall until he stopped jerking. Blood loss and the beating she had taking, took its toll and she collapsed just inside the doorway.

CHAPTER 25

As night fell silent in the small hamlet of Hayden, so did the armies of Wroughtbringer. Chaz woke from early slumber to the crashing of metal he recognized as armor. "Wake quietly, and prepare yourself for travel." The young mage slowly nudged Percy awake.

"What is it?" the groggy man asked as he sat up looking around the small room they had been given. He had barely fallen asleep when he felt Chaz's hand on him.

"I hear metal, armor metal. Either Skythane has sent troops to fetch us or…"

"Or whatever the Priestess saw has arrived." Al'daLane offered as he began gathering up the group's belongings.

"I fear the latter is more likely. We must make good our escape. From what I remember of these fine folks, they will be well under occupation. We, however, cannot afford to be kept here. I will gather the horses and meet you at the north edge of town. Do what you must to insure your friend does not alert anyone of our departure." Chaz warned the others.

"Oh, don't worry about us; we know a thing or two about sneaking out of taverns." Percy offered.

"I'm sure you do." With that Chaz cast a teleport on himself taking him to the horses he had tied behind the Inn.

"What do you suppose he meant by that?" Percy objected to his brother.

"I'm sure it was a compliment. Now get Tom ready. I have everything we need. I will follow you out and cover your escape should they take notice."

Al'daLane nudged his bother. "I am already awake. What are you two squabbling about?" Tom sat up on his elbow, his wound completely healed.

"Are you able to travel?" Al'daLane asked as he approached his friend.

"I am fine. As a matter of fact, I feel as if I have been resting in the hot springs of Carson's valley. You remember the young siren, Tatchrana? Aw, she was…"

"She was toothless as I remember her and we don't have time to argue right now. The Priestess that healed you has departed and the mage, Skythane left with us, says he hears armor," Percy cut in.

"Great! He has sent the King's men for us." Tom jumped to his feet and it was all Al'daLane could do to catch him before he broke through the door alerting everyone still slumbering in the small inn.

"If you fools are quite through making noise, there is an army amassing on the far side of town to the east. We must go and go now." Chaz reappeared in the small room. "Are you able to ride, Tom?"

"Yes. Are we sure these are not good men you see?" Tom asked.

"I have not seen their banners, but I know they do not fly the King's Colors. They have their flags tied. That, to me, means they don't want their identity known. I cannot think of a reason the King's men would disguise their coat of arms…can you?" Chaz shot back.

"Well no…but…" Tom continued.

"But if you would like to approach them, it might give us a few miles head start before they kill you. As for me, I am riding away without introducing myself. If they be friend, I am sure we will meet later…hopefully with a garrison of the King's knights beside me." Chaz blinked out again.

"I think he is ready to go. I say we go with him…Tom?" Percy looked to his friend as if to ask if they were in agreement.

"Of course we go with him. Are you daft?" Tom helped Al'daLane carry their goods to the horses. They turned their mounts to the north and raced away into the darkness. With any luck they would be in the safety of the Kingdom by next nightfall. Until then, they would have to keep a close eye on their backs. They figured the army had not come simply to conquer a single hamlet. A few hours into their escape they dropped to a slower pace, allowing for listening and for a chance to discuss plans.

"What of the towns' folk?" Percy spoke quietly in the darkness.

"They will be fine, I hope. I did not see whom the riders represented; I only can hope they were honorable men. The Hayden peoples offer no threat to any army, and they are accustomed to strangers. They will most likely be fine." Chaz offered.

"You sound almost certain there, good mage. I hope you are more certain about our direction. I believe the Kingdom lies more northwest does it not?" Tom rode up beside Chaz as they made their way into the thicker forest surrounding the Coeur D'Alene crater, a huge caldera dividing the lower half of the King's lands from the Northern Realm many of the nobles called home.

"It does. I didn't feel like giving our pursuers a destination to wait to ambush us. If you feel like you could lead us better, I will concede to your wisdom, good sir." Chaz's sarcasm was not wasted on Tom.

"I figured you knew what you were doing; I mean one does not travel with the likes of Skythane Darrow without some knowledge of survival." Tom cut back.

"We travel as equals Tom, a trait you may wish to extend to your friends here if we survive this journey."

"Are you two done? There is enough trouble behind us, need we bring in egos?" Al'daLane interrupted.

"Oh, I am fine with following our new friend here, Al'. I was just verifying our destination is all." Tom defended.

"Riders to our right." Percy's voice silenced the bickering. The group pulled up their horses and sat quietly in the dark underbrush at the edge of the crater. Gazing out through the tree limbs they spotted two riders pushing hard towards the southeast.

"Now, where do you think they are heading so fast in the dark?" Tom smirked.

"Good question. I wonder how important it is that they arrive." Chaz watched as the riders turned towards the road leading back towards Hayden. "Messengers, I would guess. But who is the sender and who is the intended receiver?"

"Well, we will never know sitting here." With that Tom drew his sword and pushed his mount out into the darkness in an intercept course with the two riders.

"Did I say we were going to find out?" Chaz looked at the brothers.

"Tom must have heard something in your voice…"Percy offered.

"Shall we assist him? He almost got himself killed the last time he played hero." Al'daLane asked calmly.

"Yeah, we better." Chaz drew up a magic missile spell and charged his mount after Tom. Percy and Al'daLane cut further ahead of the riders, cutting back through the trees hoping to come out somewhere ahead of them on the roadway stopping them as Tom and Chaz closed in from behind. On the road they could hear the hoof beats of the riders coming from the darkness. Percy conjured up the element of earth, a pile of small boulders rumbled off to the side of the road, stacking on each other they took the form of a huge stone man standing ominously beside the road as the riders rounded the corner.

The horses spooked and reared up, tossing one rider to the ground. The second man held tight to the reins and turned to run, leaving his companion to his fate. The fallen man was to his feet quickly. Weapon drawn, he prepared to fend off the rock monster. Three tiny bolts of energy slammed into his body in rapid succession, dropping him where he stood.

"You always do that. Why can you not let the elements do their job? I had this." Percy complained as the other rider rushed back into the darkness, thinking to make good his escape. They heard the brief exchange of steel followed by the sound of someone hitting the ground hard.

"Stay where you are, good sir, we simply seek information." Tom's voice shouted out.

"Who are you and by what right do you assault the ambassador of King Dominic, ruler of all the realms?" The man fell silent as Tom marched his mount to where he was standing over the man.

"Dominic, do tell, and why might an ambassador of the horrors of all that is innocent be headed in such a hurry in the pitch black, on a road four days ride on the wrong side of the boundary of Coeur D'Alene? If you are lost, our apologies, we will pay for your guard's funeral. Now if you have a message for King Darrin we will gladly deliver it for you. It is the least we can do to make up for our hasty assault." Chaz offered as he pulled his mount around circling the downed man, energy still dancing from his fingertips.

"Bah, King Darrin is no more. The young Prince will rule by sun's rise and Dominic will ride into the wide-open arms of Coeur D'Alene by sunset. If I were you fools, I would turn my tails and flee as the rest of the fallen King's cowards have done. Coeur D'Alene shall be no more and Dominic will rule the world... "The man suddenly fell silent.

"What are you saying?" Tom jumped from his mount grabbing the man by his collar and drawing back his fist. The man starred into his eyes.

"You would do well to just kill me. Our army rides this night and will sit at the gates of your precious city by nightfall tomorrow. When we do not arrive, they will send scouts, and if you are not long gone they will hunt you down like the dogs you are and kill you in a most horrific way." An evil smile stretched across the man's face.

"Bind him Tom. We will take him to the city. They have some most 'horrific' forms of torture themselves." Chaz smiled back at the man.

"I say we kill him as he requested." Percy offered as the two brothers approached.

"I would like nothing more. But if there is any truth to his words, his dead body may produce more good if it occurs in Lord Doro's presence. It will give the good Priest a chance to ask it questions we may need answers to. No, we shall take him with us. If he tries to hold us down, we simply drag him. Tie him up, Tom and let us be off. We will have to push the mounts hard if we are to beat this 'army' he speaks of."

"Hayden." Al'daLane said what they were all thinking.

"Probably, but we can't be certain. I did not see an army, nor do I think Dominic smart enough to get that many soldiers across the border without someone raising the alarm. No, I feel this man bluffs to save his hide. The man simply laughed, not too reassuring.

CHAPTER 26

Tom bound the man and tossed him across the mount he had been on. They would cut through the crater - not an easy passage, but a necessary evil at this juncture. It would cut several hours off the trip and they needed all the time they could get if the man spoke true. As the sun rose from behind the eastern mountains, the tell-tale signs that he had in fact spoke true rose into the morning sky. Smoke and way too much to be a simply chimney fire.

"Tom!" Percy called out.

"I see it." Tom responded.

"We all see it, Percy. Let us keep our eyes open and our mouths shut." Chaz silenced the group. The bound man began to laugh. Tom pulled the reins of his mount up; drawing the man next to him he quickly kicked the man in the face, knocking him out.

"The man said to be quiet." Tom smirked as the man's body fell limp across the saddle.

They rode silently for the next few hours coming up on the eastern border of the Baron's lands ten miles from the castle. From here they could see all too well that the siege had already begun. Orcs currently held the ground surrounding the kingdom.

"Since when does Dominic company with Orcs?" Tom asked as they gazed down on the battlefield.

"He is a man of little honor, Tom. He would commune with the guardians of the Hells if he thought it would insure him victory against Darrin. He is a weak man and an evil ruler Tom, do not let anything he sides with surprise you." Chaz offered as he turned away and returned to the horses. "Wake our guest, I have questions for him."

"What if he will not answer or worse, lies?" Percy asked as he cut the bindings holding the man to the saddle, his body dropping hard to the ground. With a grunt the man shook his head as he fought to clear it.

"Have you come to your senses? You wish to surrender to me now that I might ask mercy from the new King?" He held his tongue as Tom placed the edge of his sword to his throat.

"No? I have decided to let my friend here kill you after all. But I would offer you a chance to confess your Master's plans before he does." Chaz smiled and nodded to Tom as he knelt before the man. Tom pulled the blade slowly across the tender flesh of the man's throat a small trickle of blood ran down the man's neck causing him to swallow hard.

"I...know nothing of his plan and killing me will gain you nothing. I am simply a messenger." Sweat began to roll from his brow.

"You're sweating, but you were so brave last night. I guess that is just the nature of your kind. Secure in the shadows, slaying women and children, defenseless farmers and villagers. Well, although you have changed your convictions, we, I am afraid, we still feel the same as we did last evening. If you tell us, I shall leave your worthless carcass in one piece. Fail to answer me when your lips part this time, I shall allow my friend here to take your head...think about it if you wish. But be certain your decision before your lips separate. I will not repeat the offer." Chaz stood and stepped back three steps and looked at the man.

"Am I to be obligated to your kind offer? Leaving this dog's head attached just turns my stomach." Tom applied pressure to his sword, the man's body shook.

"I feel we should offer him some reprieve, Tom, I guess you could take his tongue? Seems removing that is fitting for the messenger of your enemy." Chaz snickered.

As Percy and Al'daLane chimed in with their laughter, the man vomited, falling forward in his own puke.

"Oh, that is disgusting. Tom kicked the man sideways rolling him over in the dirt. "Are you going to lap that up, DOG?" Tom taunted the groveling man.

"Please, I am truly just a messenger. I was hired to take word when the King was taken out and the Prince had seized the throne. I beg you sirs. Please. I am a family man. By the mercies of the Goddess, I beg for my life." The man choked and gagged, the four men taunting him and leering as he sobbed.

"Why would Dominic think the Prince would be any more receptive to his hand than the King would? Speak, dog, if you wish any mercy and a swift death." Tom stepped over the man raising his sword.

"He is not…not the…Prince…" The man began gasping as if choking on his own air, his face turning bright red, his cheeks swelling as he fell forward tossing around kicking and gagging loudly.

"He is cursed with a contingency. Speak quick man, he isn't who, who isn't what? "Chaz grabbed the man turning him over on his back and shaking him violently, the veins in the man's eyes had burst and blood ran from his sockets and nose. He fought to breathe, convulsions took him and he fell silent.

"Damn it! Someone did not trust our friend, and it would seem a good thing." Chaz cursed.

"For them. Kind of leaves us short though, doesn't it?" Tom asked.

"What do you think he was trying to say that they didn't want out?" Percy asked as he joined them looking down on the grotesque form that was a man only moments before.

"Don't know, but it looks like it was a painful death, I don't feel so cheated now." Tom remarked as he put away his sword and took up his horse's reins. "We need to find a way into the castle, perhaps someone there can make sense of his words…do you think he was also telling the truth about the King?" Tom mumbled as he threw his leg up, mounting his horse.

"I am hoping not Tom. But as you say, we need to get into the castle regardless. If the King has fallen, we will know soon enough." Chaz offered as he mounted up.

* * * * *

"We can use the Rogue's entrance." Al'daLane offered as he rode up beside them.

"You know the pass key?" Tom asked.

"That I do. Don't tell Shade but I have been practicing my invisibility spell." He smiled

"We have to leave the mounts out here and walk in. We shall wait for nightfall, but I for one will feel better once I am looking out-of instead of in-to Castle Coeur D'Alene." Percy said as he turned and lead his mount to a small stable built to house the Baron's mounts when they were in court.

* * * * * *

The awkward band slowly crept their way to the small culvert that marked the entrance to the Rogue's passage - a small earthen tunnel just barely four feet in height. The group would have to crouch down the whole length, two hundred yards, just to reach the outer wall opening. The gate there would be wizard-locked and unless you knew the pass phrase it would be the last gate you tried to open. As Tom and Chaz worked to open the steel grate concealing the culvert, a patrol of six Orc warriors stumbled upon the motley crew.

"Patrol!" Percy called out as he threw up a wind wall, blowing dirt to blind the Orcs as they charged up to the four men. Dust and debris flew in the face of the warrior's causing them to stop, but only briefly. With grunts and growls they quickly fought to ignore the simple nuisance and pushed forward, weapons at the ready.

From behind him, Percy heard the crackle of a lightning bolt being released from his brother; he dropped to his face on the ground and rolled out of the line of fire. The bolt raced towards the approaching threat, having the much desired effect on the three lead warriors. The bolt struck the center Orc and arched to his left and right grabbing all three in an electrifying dance, leaving them lying on the ground severely stunned when it subsided. The remaining warriors closed fast, seeing only the two mages as no real threat. Chaz's five magic missiles fell the first warrior as Tom ran from the shadows and made a quick slash across the exposed mid-section of the second one.

Percy had recovered and came up with his on magic missile spell, sending just three tiny orbs into the remaining Orc, wounding him but not nearly enough damage to stop his advance. Al'daLane stepped between his defenseless brother and the warrior, throwing a hand full of dirt and peddles he had grabbed on the fly. The dirt filled the Orc's face and eye's, causing him to drop his attack stance and try to clear his view, all Tom needed to move in and finish him off. He took three quick steps and brought his sword up, driving the tip deep into the Orc's stomach, his free hand grabbing the brute's weapon hand pulling his blade back and thrusting it back into the tough hide flesh of the Orc, causing him to shout out in agony as his knees buckled. Tom held onto the Orc's weapon hand until the beast lay still on the ground.

Tom drew his sword up and prepared to take out any of the others that might recover while Chaz and Percy worked to get the grate up. They soon heard the sound of more Orcs rushing their way.

They released the grate and as the last one entered, Tom dropped in and pulled it shut. The sound of several grunts and Orc speak, echoed down on them from above.

"We have to hurry. One of those we left alive surely saw our escape, and we won't have long before we get company." Chaz whispered out in the darkness of the tunnel.

"We at least have a little advantage in here. They can only attack one at a time and we have our magic." Percy offered. As he finished his taunt, the grate swung open and the sound of liquid splashing down from above them echoed through the darkness.

"LAMP OIL! RUN!" The smell of oil filled the small tunnel, followed by a flash as a torch fell in, lighting up the passage. The group did their best to run as the entire passage ignited in flames.

CHAPTER 27

The Crystal sword of the guardian whizzed through the air. Just as it was about to strike the unsuspecting Namsilat, he caught its glimmer out of the corner of his eye. His hand came up and the Talon appeared, blocking the strike but knocking him back into the stairwell as the second guardian moved in.

"Whoa…whoa, I assure you I am a friend here, let's not fight." Namsilat tried his best to remain calm as the two crystal warriors closed in on him. Staggering to his feet he brought his sword to guard as the second knight took its next swing. To his dismay, the glancing blow was quickly recovered and the guardian took a third swing before Namsilat had expected it. Feeling more than seeing the strike, Namsilat ducked down and rolled towards the door of the vault, bringing himself up behind both figures. With much regret and hope, he swung down on the one that had just tried to behead him. The Talon struck the magically enchanted guardian; the clashing magic sent a jolt up his arm and tossed him against the far wall, knocking the wind out of him momentarily.

"By the Goddess, this is not good." Shaking his head he got back to his feet and quickly began scanning the room for options that would hopefully not get him killed. Along the wall, to his left hung several shields. If he could just get one he could at least fend off their attacks while retreating from the vault. Thinking they would perhaps not pursue him outside the room, he released the blade and grabbed a pole arm resting against the wall to his right. Drawing it up he did his best to keep it between he and the two guardians as he maneuvered his way around them to the left. Getting his back against the wall he poked and parried until he was directly under a shield, taking the pole arm in both hands he tossed it at them as they closed.

Without turning he grabbed for a shield, and called the Talon to his hand. As his arm slipped into the strap of the shield, desperation was replaced by momentary regret. The enchantment on the shield took hold of him and against his will he moved in on the guardians. In a series of strikes beyond his skill he severed one's head and drove the Dragon's blade down the core of the second one shattering it into fragments, crackling shards scattered across the floor of the room.

Moyie and Hea'fxtrot had received word the King had fallen; they were making their way to his chamber and came up on the vault door just as Namsilat stepped from the doorway. Both men's eyes fell on the image of the shield he now wielded and in unison shouted.

"Namsilat, by the Gods, what have you done?" Moyie's hands drew his twin blades and he stepped hard in a defensive stance in front of the confused Namsilat. Hea'fxtrot brought up his staff and pointed the six headed weapon at the man now holding the Shield of Dissension, its magic swirling around his body in a frightful aura of confusion. Despite all that he would try, they knew Namsilat was powerless against the shield's magic and this was about to be ugly.

Hearing the voices, the now-possessed Namsilat turned to face the threat. The two more experienced men separated, drawing his attention in two directions. Hea'fxtrot struck first, releasing several small charges from the wand of Frost attached to the staff. As the blasts raced towards Namsilat he drew up the shield, harmlessly deflecting the bolts, but giving Moyie a chance to close for combat. Blocking the last bolt, Namsilat was met with a volley of lightning-fast strikes from the Ranger. He was able to block the first with his blade, the second and third the shield intervened, but the force with which Moyie was landing his blows pushed him back towards the vault doorway. Both men knew if they were to have a hope of ending this with little damage to the victim, they had to get the shield back inside the sanctum of the vault.

A sensation surged through Namsilat. He felt as if the attackers were trying to trap him and this would not do. Regaining his balance he threw a drawing block up in Moyie's direction, pushing the Ranger to reset. As he did so, Namsilat spun and struck at his real target. The move caught Hea'fxtrot off guard for an instant, but survival in battle is measured in those instants. The tall man blinked out of the strike. Committed, Namsilat's body staggered from the sudden lack of a receiver and the momentum of his swing. Moyie took an action he had hoped to avoid. He brought the powerful blade of Cimmerians Legacy down across Namsilat's exposed arm bearing the shield...the fight was over as his forearm fell from his body. Namsilat screamed out in agony as blood squirted from the severed stub.

"By the Gods, I was trying to stop!" He screamed at the Ranger now standing over him, still at guard. Namsilat fell unconscious from the rapid blood loss. Hea'fxtrot reappeared, grabbed the severed arm and Namsilat's unconscious body. Moyie moved in and quickly removed the shield from the severed arm tossing it back within the confines of the vault.

CHAPTER 28

"To Doro!" On command Hea'fxtrot vanished and teleported to the infirmary where Doro feverishly worked on the fading King. "Doro, you must reattach this poor fools arm, quickly it was just severed." Doro started to object, his focus was on saving the King. But he knew Thor would grant him ability to reattach the arm, saving Darrin was still uncertain.

"By Thor, how did this happen?" He grabbed the severed limb and held it to the joint from which it had been taken and called upon the God of War.

"Thor it is I, your servant Doro. Grant this poor lad his full body restored." He placed his hand over the bleeding joint and Namsilat jerked and cried out in pain as the tendons began reattaching themselves and blood once again flowed from the arm to his brain. Sweat ran from his brow, he gasped and groaned, vomiting on Doro as consciousness entered and left him several times.

"I am afraid I did it, he had taken up the Shield of Dissension." Moyie offered as he entered the room.

"How in the Hells did he come by that cursed item?" Doro turned starring at the Ranger.

"We will have to ask him when he can speak. What of Darrin?" The Elf walked to his fallen friend's side, looking down at the body barely clinging to life.

"I fear it is his heart. E'rik was with him when he fell. He said he was holding his chest, his lips have begun to turn and his breathing is fading as fast as the sanity in these walls this day. I swear it is as if all the Gods and Goddesses have abandoned Coeur D'Alene. But I have had no such warnings and Thor has been faithful to my prayers…save for the King." The priest returned to Darrin's side, standing next to Moyie.

"E'rik…E'rik isn't the Prince." Namsilat choked as the warning left his lips.

"What is he saying?" Doro turned and looked down at Namsilat lying on the floor.

"It is the shield, I am sure. Its enchantments can last in a man for days after it is taken from him." Hea'fxtrot offered.

"How do we know that? I have never heard of it being removed from a living victim until this eve." Doro shot back.

"He has a point." Moyie offered. Doro walked to the herb table and gathered several herbs. Mixing them he added Dwarven ale and had Moyie hold Namsilat as he forced the liquid down the man's gullet. Choking and kicking, Namsilat fought to break free to spit out the concoction, but Moyie held tight Namsilat fell still and Doro had Moyie release him. "Now what?"

"If it didn't kill him, he should be good as new any second." The old Dwarf teased.

"By all that is decent, what the Hells did you give me…and you, why would you cut off a man's arm? And you…well you could have tried something a little more drastic to hold me…powerful mage, huh." Namsilat began ranting. The three friends turned on him.

"What?" He concluded.

"You said something about E'rik?" Doro asked. The reaction took them all by surprise. The blade appeared in Namsilat's hand and he jumped to his feet. Thor's Hammer flew across the room. Doro's hands grabbed hard on the handle and Moyie drew the twins, stepping in to intercept the fighter should he still be cursed as Hea'fxtrot had feared.

"I told you, fools." Hea'fxtrot yelled as he blinked away from the melee.

"E'rik isn't E'rik. We have to stop him. He attacked the King" Namsilat caught sight of Darrin's body lying across the room on the table. "Tell me I am not too late, Lord Doro. Tell me he lives." Namsilat, realizing he had summonsed the Talon quickly sheathed it and stepped towards the fallen King. Moyie placed the tip of Albescence Hope in Namsilat's chest, drawing the Cimmerian's Legacy back for a quick strike. Namsilat threw up his empty hands as he stepped past the Ranger. Hea'fxtrot reappeared between the table and Namsilat as he approached, placing his staff in the man's chest.

"Be warned. I will drop you where you now stand, Namsilat Ferrie, should that blade as much as shimmer on your hip." Hea'fxtrot warned as Namsilat turned back to Doro.

"I do not know what venom he spoke of, but he bragged of your ignorance as Darrin fell from his strike."

"What strike? You saw him strike the King? Where, and with what?" Doro rushed to Darrin's side.

"It was a dagger under his arm here." Namsilat lifted Darrin's right arm as he lay on the table. The tiny puncture in the undershirt became visible. "There." Namsilat pointed.

"By Thor, the Kingdom is indebted to you. Quick, help me remove the armor." Namsilat and Doro quickly removed the Blessed armor and found the festering wound left by the poisoned dagger.

"Go find the Queen; she was with this imposter when she left here. Godspeed to you both. I fear this is unraveling in the most disastrous of ways. Whoever has plotted this attack has thought it long and hard. I pray the Gods give us guidance lest we fall prey to more deceit.

If you find the imposter, try to find out which venom he used before you slay him." Doro ushered Moyie and Hea'fxtrot out. "Did he mention anything about the poison Namsilat? Try hard to remember." Doro turned to the large shelves holding dozens of decanters of odd liquids.

"He was hissing sort of, sounded like he suddenly developed some sort of weird speech problem." Namsilat began.

"Hissing, what sort of hissing do you mean?"

Just his s's. It was like he was exaggerating them. Like

sssssword instead of sword." Namsilat tried to mimic the man's

voice.

"Do you recall the poison?" Doro urged.

"Viperssssss, yeah Vipers, is what he said with the hissss

thing." Namsilat rattled.

"Which viper, by the Gods there are too many. I could kill

him if I give him the wrong anti-venom. Perhaps they can recover

the weapon if they find the assassin. I need to know before I

introduce any form of serum to combat it" Doro began to rub his

hands over his long red beard.

"Don't you have just a fix it all thingy in here , Doro? Or do

you just hope that all your patients that get bit by snakes live to tell

you what kind it was? I thought you relied on your wisdom and the

God for that sort of divination." Namsilat felt frustrated by the

failing of the God's servant and his own.

"There are only so many serpents that call this realm their

home; if you wish to try your luck…I will have to insist you try on a

less valuable patient" the Priest shouted back.

"I am simply saying, Doro that I would think one as wise as you and as close to a God, such as Thor…I just guess I thought too highly of you." Namsilat looked at the bottles resting to on the many shelves. "All this and you can't brew a simple cure for poison." Namsilat shrugged his shoulders.

"Stay your tongue young one. I know my limitations…and I serve the God, not the other way around."

"…and those of your God as well?" Namsilat struck a nerve.

******

Just as Doro was about to explain it to him, Moyie rushed in carrying the unconscious body of Sulaunna. Blood covered most of her upper body; her face was bruised and swollen.

"We found the Queen and Hea'fxtrot brings what we assume are the remains of the assassin." Moyie laid the Queen on the table next to where Doro and Namsilat stood starring at each other. Namsilat simply smiled at the priest.

"Did you get the information from him before you slayed him at least?" Doro rushed to Sulaunna's side.

"We did not kill it; I believe your Queen put up quite the fight before succumbing to her wounds. I fear, however, that she has lost much blood." Hea'fxtrot offered as he carried the remains of the Doppelganger in and threw it on the floor at Doro's feet.

"It is as Namsilat has said…Doppelgangers!" Doro knelt down and began rifling through the blob for the weapon. His hand felt a poke; jerking back he cursed his anxious action. "By Thor, forgive me." He pulled his hand back, blood gushing from his palm.

"What have you done? You should know better. We cannot afford you to be out." Hea'fxtrot scolded the Dwarf. As they looked on, the wound healed itself and Doro's breath returned to normal. He raised his hand offering thanks as he reached back in and retrieved the dark bladed dagger.

"We are in luck, the Vipers poison has bound to the blade. I can use it to create the anti-venom." He stood and took a bowl from the shelf; dropping the dagger into it he began pouring various liquids over the darkened steel. Once he had blended the concoction he fed it to the unconscious King, knelt down and offered his prayer.

CHAPTER 29

The flames quickly threatened to engulf the band as they raced towards the wizard-locked gate into the city. Percy shouted out the verbal commands for the element of water. As he completed the spell he turned and cast it upon the tiny stream that trickled beneath their feet in the dark tunnel. The water drew together and formed up in a liquid wall between the party and the encroaching flames. Holding his ground, he concentrated on the elemental. He faced the raging wall of death as it roared through the tunnel, the flames now lighting the small tomb. The flames crashed into the watery wall, extinguishing in a loud hissing sound, sending a plume of choking smoke through the water wall but stopping the flames.

"Not perfect but I'll take it." Tom offered as a compliment, waving his hand over his face. Choking, he turned and caught up with Al'daLane and Chaz just as they reached the sealed portal. Al, you're sure you know the phrase?"

"Absolutely. Shade uses this thing at least twice a week when we are in town." Turning to the unassuming, rickety wooden door blocking the passage, he reached out with his hand tracing a large circle in the center of the door. Placing his fingertip at the lower right inner edge of the invisible circle he drew a line across the bottom. Turning his wrist upward he drew another invisible line to the top edge of the inner center, then downward connecting the Pyramid.

"Lie to any, but, to thine own self, remain always true." The door shimmered then vanished. "Shall we?" He waved his companions in.

Wasting no time, the four emerged in the Thieves Guild Hall.

"Halt, you're not Guild." The harsh voice of a large man shouted from a stool at the small bar.

"We do not have time for this. The city is under siege and like it or not, we need to go through. I assure you, my good sir, that we are no threat to your fine establishment. We bear a message for the King and you would be ill advised to interfere." Tom spoke with what authority he could.

"I know of the siege. What I don't know is how the likes of you got through the passage. Have a message for the King, do ya? Why don't you give me your tale and I will see to it that he gets it."

The huge man stood grasping a large war hammer leaning against the bar as he started towards the group, several others joined him.

"I have offered you warning. If you wish to die this day, continue to advance." Tom drew his sword and off-hand dagger. The men paused briefly, then drew weapons themselves and continued their approach.

"Tom we don't have time for this." With that Chaz, reached inside his vest and retrieved a small purse, loosed the tie string and tossed it at the men. "RUN!" was all he said as he made for the exit. Tom paused momentarily until he heard the loud buzzing the purse began to produce, and the approaching men began to scream in agony as the swarm engulfed them.

"HORNETS!" one of them cried out as they swatted at the stinging creatures, thrashing around, running into each other and trying desperately to get out of the cloud of stinging insects.

******

"Ha, ha, ha!" The band laughed as they cleared the open doorway dumping out in the lower section of the city.

"Who carries hornets?" Tom asked as they raced towards the center of town.

"Any mage worth his salt." Chaz offered as they ran through the night. The pyres of the city walls were lit giving the city a most eerie glow.

"Tom, you should go to the King. They will certainly need all the magic they can get on the walls." Al'daLane shouted as he and Percy turned towards the guardhouse.

"Easy for you to say. Just what do I tell him when I get there?" Tom shouted as the two brothers vanished into the building. "You will think of something…" they shouted back. "You always do…"

"Great…I'll think of something." Tom shook his head as he and Chaz turned and headed off towards the inner Keep.

"What do you think the traitor was trying to say that could have been so dangerous that someone would mark him with such a powerful spell?" Chaz asked as they raced up the roadway towards the guards standing at the Keep entrance.

"To be honest with you I was kind of hoping you had an idea. After all you're the one with all the experience." Tom shouted back as they closed on the gate.

"HALT, stand clear and identify yourself." The guards dropped their halberds down across the approaching men.

"It is I, Thomas of the Brothers Four. Now raise your blade and let us pass." Tom shouted not thinking to pause.

"Stop or I will defend." The man held his ground, taking a fighting grip on his weapon. Tom pulled up short raising his hands.

"Whoa…It is I, Thomas of the Deschutes. We have word for the King of great urgency from behind enemy lines." Tom waved to Chaz.

"You seem to be in the wrong place, my good fellows. Perhaps if you would be so kind as to give me your message, I will decide if the King should be bothered." A strange yet hauntingly familiar voice spoke calmly from the shadows behind the two guards. The shadowy figure began walking menacingly towards the pair as Tom drew up his sword.

"I think we can decide that for ourselves. Now if you would be so kind as to have these two brainless fools lower their weapons, I think we can forget this whole mess before it gets ugly."

"Do I know you?" Chaz stared at the figure as the moon's rays slowly worked their way up the length of his robe. He stepped closer to the edge of the shadow, stopping just before the light fell upon his face.

"I know you and that really is all that should concern you at this point. TAKE THEM!" The man shouted, putting the guards into action and causing Chaz to throw up his defenses.

With the utterance of the command word, an invisible barrier separated the attackers from him and Tom, the tips of their halberds slamming into it, causing them to reset their attack. Tom had missed the signal and began his approach. Chaz grabbed him and teleported them back to the safety of the front gate…but not before allowing him to smack his face on the barrier.

"What the fu…" Tom mumbled as he regained his composure.

"I know that voice. I thought it best if we departed." Chaz offered.

"I meant letting me smack that wall. You could have warned me." He rubbed his nose as Chaz turned and started up the stairs.

"I would have had to warn them as well, would I not?" With that he continued to the wall. They cleared the tower doorway as the first wave of the attacks began. Several men ducked for cover behind the stone machicolations of the wall just as huge stones slammed into it.

"The Hells!" Tom shouted as they dived for cover themselves.

"The attack has begun. Tom, we have to find a way into the main house. This is not a good sign, the King should be here." Chaz shouted as they stood and took to running, having to dive for cover several more times before reaching Percy and Al'daLane now standing with Tristan in the center of the wall pathway.

******

"You two get lost?" Percy yelled as they ducked behind cover.

"Got ran off, more like, there seems to be an issue with our credentials." Tom flippantly shouted over the noise of stone crashing into stone, chunks of the machicolation breaking off and flying throw the night sky. Off in the distance voices cried out as the assault took its first casualties.

"Sense, Tom. Talk sense. There is the little matter of a battle beginning here." Al'daLane shouted at his friend.

"By the Gods, how did Orcs get catapults all the way across the realm and no one saw them?" Tom shouted back as he stood to view the battlefield.

"Trolls, actually." Kia offered, standing his ground and gazing over the immense army now gathered just out of bow range on the edges of the grand city.

Tom shook his head as the magnitude of the situation unfolded before him. "Where is the King!" he shouted, looking around for some sign of their leader.

"Not so loud Tom. These men are facing a grave enough reality without being distracted by the absence of one." Tristan warned.

"Okay, so how did Orcs get huge, ugly, smelly Trolls across the realm...." lowering his voice he leaned close to the glimmering image..."I take it no one know where he is?"

"I am guessing with the assistance of very powerful magic, as to your other query I have sent runners to the main house, but none have returned. There were several Doppelgangers in the forefront of the assault; I fear there may be many still lurking in the city. I cannot leave the wall, nor can I enter the great hall or I would simply go myself. Your friends said you were on your way there…I would duck." Tristan looked over his shoulder.

Tom looked out towards the incoming stones, dropping to his stomach just as the first one smashed into the wall directly in front of them, sending large shards sailing in every direction. More screams rang out in the night.

"A little more urgency would help, Tristan, some of us are…" he dropped the comment as the priestess turned on him.

"We were headed there; someone has control of the gate guards. Tom was going to object, but I could sense he was not to be trifled with. I could feel his power and he would have used the distraction to overpower us. Surely there is another way into the Keep?" Chaz offered as he crept along the wall, keeping low.

"We could just teleport in." Percy offered.

"And have every on-edge guard pounce on you the second you appear magically within the confines of a Keep under siege …I don't think so. A front door approach is preferred here." Chaz warned.

"There is the…never mind, it might be guarded as well." Tom began. They all turned to him staring in disbelief.

"There is the garden entrance. We can get there going around the stables. There is a servant's entrance on the far side; I used to meet Kat…" Tom began to ramble.

"So you know this entrance then?" Chaz asked.

"Yes, used it quite a lot. You just have to swing around behind the stables on the East side and…" as he continued his spouting. Percy took advantage and teleported him, his brother, Chaz and the rambling Tom to the east end of the stables which he could clearly see from their vantage point on the wall.

"Wow that was quick. This way." Tom pointed to the fence that ran along the back side of the huge arena at the east end of the stables. He couldn't help but think how just two days ago they set out from here for a fun ride before a festival and now they were caught in a war, and of his good friend E'rik.

"Damn you E'rik. Where are you?" he mumbled as he drew his sword and lead the small band off into the darkness.

CHAPTER 30

Doro had just finished praying over the Queen; administering all the healing he could at this point, he turned to inform the group that all they could do now was wait. Suddenly two guards raced in carrying the unconscious and bloody body of Skythane Darrow.

"By the Gods, can this get any worse?" Doro cursed, knowing it was not a good question at this time. Leroy rushed in.

"Where is everybody? There is a war going on!" Leroy let his question roll off when his eyes fell on the three bodies lying about the infirmary. All three of the men moaned out in unison as he entered the room and paused. Hea'fxtrot threw out his left hand smacking Doro firmly on the back of his head...THWAACK!"

"You had to ask." He scolded the shorter man as they stood and starred at what...and who, it would appear now would control the fate of all of Coeur D'Alene.

"What...why is everyone staring at me?" Leroy began waving his index finger, then his head followed, then his voice... "No, no, oh no, you are all fools if you think...I cannot...you have to wake one of them Doro, it's your job."

Leroy began walking from table to table. "Where is E'rik? He is next in line and Father was going to…" The huge man stood holding the massive weapons of thunder to either side of him; he had donned in his battle armor, an ominous sight to behold.

"Such is life, my dear Leroy. It would appear that the Gods have chosen you to defend your Father's throne. It is not the ideal situation I can assure you, for any of us. But I am a man of faith and action." Doro did his best appear calm.

"If I am reading this right, it is a matter of action here, not faith." Doro calmly stepped over, taking his position next to the now ruling member of the House of Coeur D'Alene. "How say you, gentlemen?" He flipped the mighty Maul of Thor, letting the tip of the handle rest on the marble floor, the head standing a good foot over his own.

"I pledged my swords to this house many years ago, I will not remove it now." Moyie Spring took his place on the left side of Doro. Hea'fxtrot shook his head and gave his nervous laugh as he raised his staff and stepped towards the trio.

"We're in serious trouble; you all know that…right? I mean, I'm not saying anything we aren't all thinking here." He stood next to the others. Holding his staff at guard he tapped it on the floor signaling his agreement.

"I must tend to the fallen here, Leroy. I will leave the Kingdom to your hands, and if you need me I will be by your side. I would guess at this point Moyie and Hea'fxtrot can join you in the planning room." The old Dwarf did his best to put his hand on the younger man's shoulder, falling short he patted him on the right side of his chest. "We can do this. Just remember to hold your anger until it is truly needed. A great battle requires a focused mind." He starred into the Barbarians eyes.

"I shall do my best Lord Doro, but the rage already boils within me. We need to get word out of the castle; we only have two thousand warriors inside the walls. While the walls hold, we are balanced, but they are only stone and eventually they will be breeched. I would feel much more comfortable with a little more flesh to fill the hole." Calmness fell over him, his red eyes slowly turning back to a softer more focused blue.

"I can slip out, but I hate to take my swords out of you arsenal my liege." Moyie offered.

"There will be time for these thoughts, let us retire now to the planning room. We have more information there to assist us in these matters." Hea'fxtrot guided them out of the room. "...and Lord Doro can do better without our banter."

"I can get out of here." Namsilat mumbled leaning against a table across the room. They all stopped and look at him, and then they turned to Doro.

"I have done what I can for him. The Gods have already done him a great service, and I would think him more grateful and less demanding." The Priest gave Namsilat a stern glare.

"I am most grateful, to you and your God's, good sir. I have heard of potions that will allow the most fragile to stand and fight. Might you have such potions here?" Namsilat slowly rose up.

"I might, but it is too soon in this battle to start draining the potion supply." Doro's concern for the young man showed through.

"I am not asking for the storehouse, Doro. Many will die this day, if I am to be one...so be it. I release you of any responsibility in that."

"That is awfully generous of you my young friend..." Doro started to object.

"Let him go, Doro. He is a grown man. If he thinks he can sneak past that army, let him try. Either way we lose nothing. And you yourself know the feeling of sitting by and watching a fight." Moyie interjected.

"Tell me not what I feel, Moyie. You know all too well how I feel about this thing called war."

"Doro, I understand your hesitation, but I believe I have a better mount then anyone here. I doubt I shall go unnoticed, however." Namsilat smiled at the group.

"If it were not for the protections placed on the city we could just have Ish teleport to the valley, or even Hea'fxtrot. With it up, none can enter or exit."

Doro grumbled. Like it or not they needed someone to do exactly what Namsilat had stepped up and done. "I will give you two doses of the revitalizing potion, take one before you begin, it will last but four hours. After that you had best hope you are free of any pursuers you pick up. Save the last potion for your return…if there is one." The old Dwarf wandered off, returning quickly. "Here, drink only half. Remember you need the remainder for the return." Doro handed Namsilat the vial.

303

"If I drink it all at once, will the magic last longer?" Namsilat asked as he uncorked the small bottle of liquid. He held it to his lips and drank it down in one large gulp.

"Yes, but don't! You are a fool man, that potion will if nothing else, make you restless. Your focus will be all over the place making it impossible for you to stay in the saddle." Doro offered.

"You assume I intend to ride in a saddle." Namsilat offered as the potion flooded through his body. "I feel great, I will travel to SilverLeaf and return with Airapal and her warriors."

He turned and walked out onto the balcony looking down over the city. Fires lined the top of the city walls, several more burned in the center of town. Guards worked feverously fortifying the various gates separating the neighborhoods of Coeur D'Alene. Catapults and Trebuchets were being move towards the front half of town, carts of boulders and giant three foot arrows were following close behind. Columns of soldiers marched to their respective locations. Namsilat looked up into the dark night sky; stars were just beginning to shine. The moon shone brightly over the eastern mountains. "Strange. I guess I never thought such peace could exist during such great conflict...Gentlemen." With that he took a bow and raced down the outer staircase leading into the center of the stables arena. Walking quickly to the middle of the dirt arena he drew the Talon…gazing into the handle he called out.

"FireClaw I need your help."

* * * * *

Four hundred miles away, through valleys and over mile high mountain ranges, the grand Red sailed through the Columbia River gorge, fishing and basking in her splendor when the voice beckoned to her.

"Of course you do, but what is that to me?" she thought back, gazing out at him through her mind's eye.

"I just need a…I need to get to the SilverLeaf valley, and I need to get there fast." Namsilat had never asked a Dragon for a favor, and at their last meeting she had warned him to stay away from her lair. He had spent much of the last two seasons with Airapal and her people in the SilverLeaf valley. She and the Sages had shared their knowledge of what it was to be in possession of a Kindred blade. How, when a Dragon chooses a Kindred it is their way of marking the Kindred by a magical gift fitting of their class.

That often the gift would allow the Dragon to call upon the Kindred when it desired something, or had need of their services in some fashion. What he had heard was that it bound her to him.

"So have your little friend cast you there. I am feeding, and need I remind you it is not good to interrupt the Supreme when they feed?"

"My little friend cannot cast me anywhere right now. I am in the King's city and there is a barrier over it that prevents such actions. I need, I need a ride…from you!" Namsilat struggled with just how to speak without sounding desperate. He could see the mighty beast using the stone to inspect the city.

"I see there is. Why not have the good King drop the shield and let the small one use his magic?" Gazing through the stone, FireClaw began to plan how to bring more of the human's land into her view. "I see there seems to be an awful lot of Orcs there. Has the Human king thrown in with Oshta Bah'? I would hate to think that he would be so foolish." Her words were taunting and Namsilat knew it.

"So you see the problem and why he cannot just drop the shield. I need to get to the Elvin people and ask their aide for the

King. How fast can you get here?" The roaring laughter in his head did little to settle Namsilat's fear.

"Oh you are a funny one. I could have already been there. I however sense that Oshta Bah's Pa warriors are not the only threat your King faces. There is a great amount of evil in your presence. I fear that you have gotten in on the wrong side of that battle. No worries. I will retrieve my Talon once the fires die down." She cooed at him with an eerie calm.

"I am your Kindred; surely you know that connects us by your doing. I have a need and you are so bound to provide me your assistance." He spoke boldly, yet ignorantly and she let him know it.

"I WHAT? Presume not, frail creature that my gift to you in any way grants you dictating to me. If I chose to summons you, not that I ever could need your assistance, yes. But it does not work the other way. Did the Elves tell you different? I doubt it. They are at least…wise regarding the supreme. No, I fear you have assumed much. Now I have fish to feast upon if we are through here.

"What if I offer you a payment?" Namsilat let his mouth over run his brain once again.

"What have you, that I would perceive as worthy of allowing you to ride upon my back? Lie not to me Half-Elf," her eye filling the entire stone.

"I have an item of the greatest evil. An item that any of your race would envy the one that possessed it." He was already in, might as well make it good.

"Oh, show it to me. I will decide its worth." She starred into the man's eyes.

"I will show it to you, and give it to you, once I have returned from the SilverLeaf valley. Not a moment before."

"You have no such item; you play a foolish game, creature. Be off now. I grow annoyed." She turned her back on the gem and flew away from him.

"I'll not go. And annoyed? You have not felt the breeze of annoyance I shall heap upon you, until the Orcs take this stone for themselves, or you assist me. And I know you can hear every word I speak. I have nothing more to do while we await the attack. I swear I have such an item, an item one such as you can use for your most sordid pleasures. It is enchanted with the contradiction magic that will make wise men fools." Namsilat tried one more lure. Just as she was about to fade from his sight, she turned abruptly and drew his sight back to her eye.

"Oh really, is this item perhaps a shield small one?" Her interest should have made him think twice…but…

"It is. Do you know of it? I have felt its power and I swear I do possess it." He committed himself, and had just offered property of the King as if it were his own. "But, it will remain out of your grasp until you have completed my request."

"And should you perish in this upcoming battle, how shall I retrieve my payment?"

"I will reveal the location to you. Surely a few Orcs and several dead things could not keep you from your possession once it is yours?" He baited her.

"You do not know how right you are. Did the Elves mention to you that in accepting my gift, that you granted me certain abilities to control you?" She teased now.

"I would jump from a balcony before I would simply allow you to take the item without helping." He hoped. Her sinister laughter did little to raise his spirit. "You toy with me; you are truly evil as the Elves have spoken. I shall await your arrival then, I

assume we have a deal?" Namsilat sheathed the Talon.

CHAPTER 31

"Did I hear you correctly, Namsilat? Did you just offer that beast the Shield of Dissension? A possession currently in the King's vault…BECAUSE IT BELONGS TO THE KING!" Doro was shaking when he caught his breath.

"I did, and do not worry, I will make it right by him. She is not an easy creature to deal with and I got desperate. We need the Elves help, do we not? The King and Queen are indisposed and one heir is missing, another wounded and the fate of all Coeur D'Alene rests in the hands of what looks like a Barbarian? I believe that speaks to desperation"

Namsilat threw up his hands. He did not comprehend the situation as well as Doro did, but he had described it fairly accurately. But even Doro would not presume to bargain with the King's property. And the shield was in the vault for very good reasons; FireClaw the Red was one of those very good reasons.

* * * * *

Four hundred miles away the giant Red caught the updrafts and sailed high into the blue sky. It would take her only moments to soar to the Kingdom of humans, but she had no need to rush. She would take her time and, in her grand fashion, make an appearance. She turned north and glided across the vastness of the gorge, herd animals running beneath her shadow. Crossing the great plains of the Northeastern boundaries, she caught a glimmer of magic below her, strong magic. Slowing, she circled back, and looking through her eyes of truth she saw them. Orcs, thousands of them, cloaked under an inadequate shield of concealment. On any other day she would have perhaps ignored them, but not likely, for they were too close to the lands she called her own. And other than humans, Orcs were her least favorite of the created.

She could sense they had noticed her sudden change in direction, and like so many prey animals they froze, hoping beyond hope that she had not spotted them. So the game begins, her favorite sport. She sailed just beyond the range of their weapons and set her wings, landing in a cloud of dust. For her own twisted pleasure she turned her back to them, taunting them to come out of their presumed safety.

She sat for several moments, but none would take the bait. With a mighty roar she leapt into the sky. Initially hovering thirty feet above the ground, she set her course directly over them, sailing like gentle death out of their reach. Turning skyward, she pushed her great wings and gained speed, quickly fading from their sight. Soaring above the sagebrush covered plains she gathered velocity until there was no more sound around her. Holding her speed she turned, dipping down to ground level and racing towards the unsuspecting army.

Thirty miles away and unaware of her approach, Oshta-Bah, ruler of the lower Wasteland Orcs, gave the signal for his army to take up their march. They had thrown in with their warring brothers from the eastern wastes across the Dragon Scales. Despite warnings from his Shaman, he had committed the strength of his entire army to the war Dominic of the Humans wished to wage against the northern King. He and LaBatosh had devised a plan to finish off Coeur D'Alene and then turn on Dominic's warriors before they could regroup, thus annihilating the weaker human race from the realm.

His infantry had just gathered up their gear and started to march again when the fires from Hell rained down on the center of the huge army, now hunkered down in the open. Silence was quickly replaced by the agonizing cries of the dying. The very ground beneath them boiled and turned to glass as several attempted hopelessly to run from the flames.

Oshta-Bah had just mounted Octavoos, his huge desert Warg, when the flames descended. Octavoos had a natural defensiveness to fire, however, Oshta-Bah did not and the flames consumed the Orc sitting in his saddle atop the huge beast. Octavoos let out a loud thundering howl of pain as his master's flesh turned to liquid and ran down the beast's sides. Oshta-Bah felt the initial heat from the flame, but the death came swiftly and before he could hope to flee his blood boiled within his veins and his eyes exploded in their sockets. The field was ablaze. Pa warriors raced desperately to make good their escape. Hoping the red Death would devour the wounded and allow them to bolt.

At speeds too fast for the lesser creature's eyes to follow, FireClaw had descended upon the caravan of Orcs, releasing her breath like a flowing stream as she zipped over the center of the mass. Her fiery ball of internal fuel ignited everything and scorched the ground beneath it. The tiny creatures burst into flames and began running in terror. She felt a great joy well up inside her as she flew away, knowing they would cower there in fear of her return. She figured it would give her plenty of time to fetch the Half from the castle and return before they would decide their next step. Knowing Orcs, retreat would be their choice, but either way she had had her fun. Now traveling at a greater speed than she had intended, she closed on the human Kingdom rapidly.

Her eyes fell upon the army surrounding the human kingdom just as her sensitive ears heard the warning horns sound out her approach. The Orcs here had been on high alert, and though concealed mostly by the darkness, their lookouts had spotted her silhouette in the night sky as she raced towards them. At once they mustered their defenses and brought up their long range weapons. Alongside the Orcs, Giants took up massive spears and Trolls were armed with boulders.

If FireClaw had time she could strike them as well for her own pleasure, but she had not come here to assist the human King, if only for her own delight. As her giant frame cleared the army and she set her wings to slow her approach, somewhere in the darkness a foolish Orc commander perceived her arrival as a signal for the attack on the castle. The charge was given and columns of Orcs,

Giants and Trolls, and a regiment of Warg riders moved towards the now heavily defended walls of Coeur D'Alene. Confusion is a bad thing on the frontline and it had just set in on the army of LaBatosh, war chief of the Eastern Wasteland's mighty army. He was quick to respond, but it would take a toll on his army.

As FireClaw raced undistracted over the screaming sirens of the Orcs, her arrival caused a similar reaction from the human lookouts. Warnings filled the night from around the upper walls. Several Ballista bolts whizzed by her…suddenly a familiar scent caught her attention, her internal defenses automatically engaging. There was a trespasser in her domain, and she flapped her wings several times to loft higher into the skies above the human city. Was this a trap?

She surveyed the skies. Nothing. Then the scent began to fade. Was it possible that another Supreme had taken an interest in these skirmishes? Satisfied they had departed, she glided back towards the human city. Locking her wings she dropped her massive frame towards the center of the arena. "Obviously, HALF, you did not warn your companions of my coming!" She filled the cavern of Namsilat's mind with her harsh rebuke.

"So sorry. If you had actually told me you accepted my offer they would have been told." he screamed back in his mind. He could see her huge form as she slowed for her approach, wings flapping, sending dust and debris into the night air below her as she let herself fall on top of the grand stables, shattering several of the roof joists, huge chunks of plaster shingles tumbled down around the building. "Can you be more careful, these people are already having a problem with your arrival, destroying things isn't going to help me convince them you are a friend."

"I am not their friend, Half; you would be doing them a grave disservice if you convince them otherwise." She lowered her head towards the balcony Namsilat now stood perched on, awaiting her answer before she arrived. Her snarls and growls filled the air as she hissed out a warning to approaching warriors. Just as it appeared they were to strike, a booming voice from the darkness stopped them.

"Halt guards, this beast is not to be attacked, it has come to our aide. Cease and hold your weapons." The stout Barbarian stepped from the shadows. At first the men paused, but then a second voice commanded them to continue.

"He is not your master. Attack the foul creature lest it interferes with the Master's plan. Strike it down and take the fool as well." The hooded image appeared behind the men and they took up their attack. Two closed on Leroy, while three others moved to engage the Dragon.

"We should be going, Half. If these fools push my hand, this tiny building will be the least of the destruction I will bring here." She lowered her head bringing her nose a few feet away from the edge of the balcony.

"Seriously, can you not get just a tad closer here?" Namsilat looked at the huge nostril and the three foot leap to it, then down. The thirty-five foot fall was more than he cared to try to survive.

"I suggest you don't look down and....JUMP!" Her voice startled him into action and he leaped, his first foot catching the inside of her nostril, his hands grasping desperately for holds as she leaped back into the night sky. A voice shouted out from below as she sped away.

"Yeah, you go on, I got this." Leroy watched in disbelief as the creature he had just assisted left him to his fate.

CHAPTER 32

Leroy turned and faced the now five attackers and the image of Garrett.

"So, it would appear that you are not whom you presented yourself to be, dark one. But no matter, I will find who holds your leash and have my revenge." With that Leroy raised his weapons and charged. Swinging up with his right hand he caught the first guard dead on, the impact crushing the steel plate helm, sending the lifeless body sailing back towards the gate wall. His left hand came down meeting the second man square in the face, the resounding echo of steel on steel signaled the end of a second attacker. The man's body fell forward into a crumbled mass. Leroy threw back his arms, thrust his chest forward.

"Come on Cowards!" He brought the mighty hammers crashing together before him, sparks of energy shot into the darkened air around him. As he drew the hammers back a bright yellow arc flashed between them. Whirling the right hammer back, he lashed it forward like a whip sending the arc racing towards the dark mage. The energy smashed into the wall of protection the image of Garrett had cast when he saw the huge man appear. The bolt hit, spread out and engulfed the mage, then dissipated harmlessly into the air.

"Perhaps another time." The mage taunted as he quickly vanished, leaving three more guards to deal with the son of Darrin.

"I hate mages." Leroy spat at him as he vanished, then turning slowly he met the three attackers as they rushed him. The first guard swung his halberd at Leroy as he closed. A loud clanking sound, followed by the sound of rushing wind was all the man heard as Leroy's left hand hammer blocked his swing, then the right hand rushed in striking him on the left temple. The grotesque sound of his skull imploding filled the air. The other two attackers paused.

One man stepped to Leroy's right, holding the tip of his weapon out as if to hold the huge man at bay. His comrade rushed in from the left, swinging down towards Leroy's legs. Keeping his eyes focused on the man to his right, Leroy simply raised his foot and quickly stomped down, catching the weapon under his steel boot. The wooden handle snapped and the man staggered backwards holding the stump, which he tossed aside and ran off towards the gate. As he cleared the gate, Leroy threw Leroy's Boom stick, sending it soaring at the coward, the thunder clap exploding on impact, causing the man still facing him to fall to the ground deafened. The body of the man struck by the hammer took flight and sailed some thirty feet before slamming into the gate wall and falling limp to the ground.

Leroy calmly stepped over to the man lying on the ground holding his ears. Seeing the huge shadow looming over him, the guard turned his face up slowly. Leroy stood smiling down on him, his left hand extended out, catching the hammer as it returned to him. Holding the hammer high, he drew the man's attention to it; in a flash he smashed the man's head into the ground with Ishtar's Messenger. It was over.

Leroy tossed back his head, throwing his arms back as wide as they would go and screamed into the night.

"Let them come!"

* * * * *

Namsilat fought desperately to get some hand hold on the huge beast as she raced skyward. He hadn't thought about how one actually rides a Dragon.

"If you don't sit still soon, I'm going to land and you can walk from here," FireClaw warned as she settled into a level flight a thousand feet above the Coeur D'Alene landscape.

"Where exactly is here?" Namsilat asked as he settled into the cleft of her nostril just above her upper lip.

"We are a short distance from the great River. We should be crossing into the human lower lands anytime now. A short distance from SilverLeaf for me, several days walk for you." She turned her head downward allowing him a better view and upsetting his seating. Looking down he quickly realized he did not care for flying.

"Can you just hold yourself still? I didn't need to see our height. I fear I am not as comfortable with this flying thing as you and the magi seem to be." He tightened his grip and tried to reestablish a place for his butt.

"I find it is not so much the flying that terrifies the earth-bound; it is the falling that causes them discomfort." With that she folded her wings and let herself begin to fall towards the earth. Just above the ground she spread her wings and soared across the surface. Namsilat screamed at the top of his lungs.

"Do not ever...ever do that again. We have a deal, remember." He tried to conceal his pleading as a demand.

"You have a deal, and might I remind you that in your species I am considered by many as the Devil. What sort of fool makes a deal with a Devil, Halfling?" She curved her wing tips, sending them climbing high into the night skies once more.

"I am not a Halfling, for one thing. And I did not make a deal with you; I offered you payment in exchange for a ride. What sort of 'Supreme' allows herself to be ridden like a common horse, for a simple shield?"

Namsilat busied himself tying his belt around one of the smaller scales covering the side of her nose. He had just cinched it around his waist again when she responded as he thought she would. In a quick jerk she tossed herself skyward, then turned and raced towards the ground. The force of the air passing by them soon took his breath away; his hands clung tight to her nostril. At tree top level she threw her body into a spin. Namsilat held on, but his stomach cared little for the ride. His head began to feel fuzzy and just as he thought he would surely pass out, she leveled off and landed. Hoping the worst over, Namsilat fought to catch his breath and clear his head. The mighty creature began shaking her head violently like a dog trying to shake off an annoying cat attached to its face.

"You will get off of me NOW!" She threw her head back, inhaled deeply; there was a bright flash as the internal furnace lit the fumes of her exhaled breath. He felt the heat grow intense, releasing his belt he allowed himself to fall to the ground. He came up Talon in hand. The Red turned on him, her wings up, her head thrust forward. Before he could even think, her right foot came to rest above him like a giant cage. She lowered her face to her claw.

"You are a fool, Half-Elf, it is no mere shield you have offered me, it is perhaps one of the strongest items ever created by the Drow lord herself. I knew you had no clue as to its origin. As for the ride, I care little for your presence, you annoy me no more on my back than you do in my mind. But be clear here frail one, I do not need to do you any favor, now that I know the resting place of the Drow shield, I need only go retrieve it. If you can remain silent for the rest of your short flight, I will fulfill my agreement. Speak again and I will make you a memory…do you understand me?" Her eyes never blinked.

Namsilat simply nodded no need to piss her off. She slowly lifted her claw allowing him to climb back on her and they took to the air. He gazed out over the dark landscape below them; small fires littered the land in various locations. She raised her right wing and her body turned left away from the moon. Turning her head slightly he could now see the Spire of Mount Hood glowing in the night sky. She made a pass around the mountain, flying lower as she came around the west side and began her journey out over the plush forest into the SilverLeaf valley. She turned south up the winding tail of the Sandy River. Namsilat couldn't help but think of the Halfling village and little Becca. He strained his eyes to try and see the remains of it as they sped over the swamp at lightning speed. As Tigard fell behind them, the thick forest of the SilverLeaf opened up beneath.

"I guess I should have asked if you know where we are going, right." When his words left his lips, his hands flew to his ears to block her loud screech filing the night air. "No words." He mumbled holding his ears.

"I was letting your friends know I come in peace and to stay their attacks. It is a courtesy, something you might try before invading someone's home." She scolded him as she set her wings and began hovering hundreds of feet above the ground, circling as if searching for something.

Within minutes there were several horns blowing from the canopy below them. "They have accepted my gesture; I will not take you into their city. My presence tends to confuse those that still bear harsh feelings about supposed 'wrongs' by my kind. There is a large lake on the edge of their city, do you know it?"

"Well. Airapal and I spent many a fine evening walking…"

"I will take that as a yes. They will send a boat for you. Try not to get eaten by any of the beasts that might be watering there." With that she descended rapidly, soaring just over the glowing lights of the Elven city. Shouts and screams filled the air as she rushed over. Setting her wings she glided into the shore line and landed with the grace of a much smaller creature.

"Speak not of our conversation, Namsilat Ferrie. The humans would have mixed feelings about one who rides a Dragon…and the Elf Priestess is the only one that needs to know why I came here. I will take your word of honor on this matter." She turned her face to him her right eye looked into his eyes.

"You have my word." He gave a bow. "But you're not leaving, right?" He could only stand and watch as the huge beast flapped her mighty wings twice and vanished into the darkness. "How am I supposed to get back?" He slapped his hands to his thighs.

"Are you speaking to me, master Namsilat?" It was the voice of Tyrun, Airapal's newly appointed WoeTeaf Captain who spoke as his small barge pulled along the bank of the Shimmering Lake.

"No, Tyrun…I was talking to myself. And haven't I told you not to call me master. It's Namsilat, just Namsilat. Is Airapal awake? There is a war building in the human lands and they need your help." He stepped into the small Elven boat and they raced back across the shimmering waters.

CHAPTER 33

Leroy looked around for any more threats, his hammers still glowing with electricity. A movement at the far end of the stable grounds caught his keen eye. Turning to his left he rushed to intercept.

"Are you sure this leads to an entrance into the castle, Tom." Chaz whispered as they made their way through the darkness.

"Yes, yes…I told you I used to meet…" Tom began

"Yes is all we need, Tom." Percy offered as they inched along. As he spoke, Tom suddenly froze, bringing the group to a halt.

"What is it?" Chaz asked as he brought his spell up.

"That." Tom responded as he brought his sword up to guard. Standing in the center of the arena was a huge brute, lightning bolts dancing between his hands.

" HALT! STEP FORWARD AND BE RECOGNISED!" the voice boomed out. Percy and Al'daLane brought up spells as well. They had never seen such a huge mage before and they were certain if he were in the King's accompaniment they would have met.

Thinking they had some advantage in unknown numbers, Percy slipped into invisibility.

"Why don't you come in and kiss my magical little…" Chaz taunted.

"Really?" his companions moaned in the darkness.

"CHAZ, by the Gods, is that you. Why are you sneaking around? There is a war brewing. There are many here that would have attacked you for lurking in the shadows. Come, we have enemies at our door." The big man relaxed his posture as Tom and the others breathed a sigh of relief.

"You could just tell us he is friend next time." Tom shoved the smaller mage as he walked out into the arena.

"Big man, we must see the King. There are enemies coming in from the Badlands and I fear they have the Prince." Chaz put his hand on Leroy's shoulder.

"Neat trick…well I guess you can see him. Not much he can do though. He has been poisoned. The Queen was attacked and lies unconscious in the infirmary. And E'rik, well, he wasn't what he appeared and then there is ME!"

The huge man gave a sarcastic smile. All Chaz could do was stand in shock. "Yeah, how do you think I feel? I go to the gates; my men must see their leader. Doro is with the fallen and he says the King should recover."

"Not that I want to know the answer to this and don't take it wrong…but what of Sky?" Chaz asked hesitantly.

"Went and got himself shot. He lies in the infirmary as well." Leroy smiled his nervous smile again.

"You mean you are ruling the armies?" The fearful group muttered from the edge of the stables.

"Yup, me and the Goddess." Leroy pointed skyward with Ishtar's Messenger shaking his head as he looked back towards the front gates. "And if that ain't bad enough for ya, there is a black mage running around inside these walls. Ran off when I challenged him…mages are, and don't take this the wrong way…cowards." He smiled at the group lurking behind the shadows of the stable.

"Not all." Tom stepped out into the moonlight. "But most." Tom added his agreement as he joined the other two men standing in the center of the arena.

"I know of the dark mage. We had a little run in with him. That is why we were going through the service entrance when you spotted us. What is this you are saying about E'rik not being who he said he was? Did you and the others find him?"

Chaz began to look around nervously. This was not looking good, and he worried if the Barbarian leader could command a group of non-raging warriors. Brave as they may be, they do not possess the ability to put their own safety aside in an insane battle rage. And Leroy could only contain his rage so long and they both knew it. No, this night was shaping up poorly for the city of Coeur D'Alene.

"We found what we thought was him, turned out he, it, was a Doppelganger. Attacked the King and then set against the Queen. From the looks of it, she killed it but paid a heavy price in blood to do it." Leroy was now swaying back and forth and Chaz could see the agitation growing with in him.

"Leroy, I know you don't need me to tell you this, but seeing that Skythane is not here...you need to breath." Chaz looked into the big man's eyes; they had already begun to turn red and glowed slightly in the moon light.

"Huh? Oh, I'm alright. Just need to get to battle. I am sure I can find a use for this energy. If you must see them, I shall be at the front." He turned and began walking south towards the center of the city.

"Leroy, they are good men and they will do right by you. But you must remain calm. You cannot rule them as you would your own warriors." Chaz shouted out as the big man walked off into the darkness.

"What now, the traitor was telling the truth and it seems we are in dire straits. I cannot believe the fates of the entire realm are now in his hands." Tom said as Leroy faded from view.

"I can still hear you…" Leroy shouted back over his shoulder.

* * * * *

"We have to get to the infirmary. Doro will know what our next step is to be. If there is a silver lining in all this, it is good to have the God of War's favorite Priest on your side. If we are to fight, I for one would not have it the other way around." Chaz waved Percy and Al'daLane out of the shadows.

"Who was the Dragon rider anyone recognize him?" he asked as the pair joined them.

"That would be Namsilat, but I am not sure I would call him a Dragon rider. We ran a little quest with him a couple of years ago up in the snow caps. He seems to have picked up a new companion though, as I recall the beast had threatened to kill him when they last met." Tom explained as they raced towards the castle doors.

"Well again, I would rather it was for us than against us." Chaz shouted as he pulled open the huge doors and ushered the others in.

"Yeah, I thought for sure it was here to join our foe. When it first flew over the city I was sure this was over. If it is the same beast, she is a mighty foe in and of herself. With the King's army behind her, this fight would be short at best." Percy said as he raced into the foyer.

"Where do you think they are off to?" Chaz asked as he led the group up the huge curved staircase leading to the upper halls of Castle Coeur D'Alene.

"My guess would be the SilverLeaf Elves." Tom offered.

"SilverLeaf? They are days away, by the time they arrive it may be to light the funeral pyres." Chaz shook his head as they cleared the upper deck.

The upper halls of Castle Coeur D'Alene were an armory on their own. Shields from several loyal houses hung, mounted above exquisite suits of armor gifted to the Kings of Coeur D'Alene of the 500 years of its existence. Racks of weapons, some magical, and many non-magical but finely crafted, lined the long corridor framed with beautiful tapestries and painting. Four giant chandeliers hung from the arched ceiling, lit by the sun during the day through ports built into the painted scenes that graced the entire ceiling forty feet overhead. Magical spheres created the light at night and on dark dreary winter's days when the sun stayed hidden.

"I guess I never really noticed the beauty here before." Tom uttered as he turned several times taking in the view as they ran down the huge hall way.

"You noticed. You kept trying to get Darrin to gift you a weapon, Tom." Al'daLane shouted as they reached the end of the corridor and turned into the Infirmary.

"Never hurts to ask…" Tom cut short his statement as his eyes fell on the somber scene of the fallen now in Doro's care. "By the God's, its true then?" he mumbled as he walked into the silent room.

"You think we were all sharing the same nightmare, Tom?" Chaz asked as he approached Doro. "Is there any word on their chances, Lord Doro?"

"I am afraid not, nothing promising anyways. I have treated master Skythane, but it is up to Ishtar if he is to rejoin us. I cannot intervene for him. As for the King, his blood was thick with the Vipers poison by the time I found out what it was. If Namsilat hadn't come around soon enough to warn me, I would have let him die, thinking it was his heart. Her Majesty's wounds are simple enough, but again the Goddess must decide to release her to us or she will surely succumb to them. I have done all I can for her I fear." The Priest shook his head and looked around the room.

"What of the armies, has anyone gone to call them back to the castles defense?" Chaz asked.

"I do not know. Moyie and Hea'fxtrot are in the war room looking over options. Leroy is in charge of the King's men until one of these regains consciousness. I hope it's sooner rather than later. Leroy is a hell of a warrior, I do not know of his leadership abilities however. You would know better than I on that matter. Kia and Mistress Tristian are still on the wall and will assist him I am sure, but he must accept the help or it is useless. If he loses his temper and rages, we will most certainly lose him as well.

These are perilous times, my friends. We have not even the time to assess the threat, let alone consider actions. It is good to know what or who one faces before you respond." The old Dwarf walked calmly around the infirmary checking on his patients.

"We have run into a dark mage and Leroy says he had an encounter with him as well. With the protection cloak over the city he is as trapped as we are. Perhaps Hea'fxtrot can track him. He may be the first step to find out who our attacker is."

"Percy, you and Al'daLane stay here and assist Master Doro, Chaz and I will join up with Moyie and Hea'fxtrot. If we can locate this mage, perhaps we can turn this around or at least have a starting point for our response.

Master Doro." Tom gave a bow as he and Chaz left the infirmary.

Epilogue

Renna had escorted Darrin and E'rik to the vault. She had taken her leave to go to the mage's guild to replenish spell components and to check up on her arrant spy. As she made her way along the corridors of the Castle Coeur D'Alene, she was stopped suddenly as a smoldering mass of goo appeared before her, bubbling and eating away at the hard tile flooring.

"Gadrash!" Renna felt the defense of the Rose fall over her as she conjured up her own protections against any evil that might be lurking. "Gadrash…appear." She commanded the tiny being back from the twisted nether of the lower plane. The naked essence appeared shimmering undefined before her. "Gadrash, what happened, why are you formless?" she demanded an answer.

"*Master, I have been rejected from this plane. It will take me a time to reform…unless you would release me and re-summons my essence back?*" The Imp saw freedom taunting him from the edge of his realm.

"You would like that wouldn't you, you ungrateful, foul demon. I have not got time to trifle with the likes of you. I have commanded you here and you have not obeyed. Do not toy with me like some first-season trickster you can manipulate with your lies. If you will not take a form, I shall find one and confine your essence to it." Renna began looking around the corridor for an insulting receptacle for her arrant Imp.

"Please master, I will form presently..." the Imp's essence blinked several times coming to form just as Renna picked up a small Jade figurine of a pig from a table next to her. Standing before his master, the Imp snarled as she taunted him with her offering. "I am here master, at your demand.

"No more trifling Gad...I will command you into this vessel and inscribe your full name on its base for the entire world to shout out at every reading. Do you understand?" She waved the green swine at the lesser demon.

"Yes, master. I am yours to command and deal as you see fit, your humble servant begs your forgiveness." He fell silent and his eyes dropped to her feet.

"Now speak of what you saw before I send you back for more." Renna starred sternly at the small creature as he began to tell his tale...

"A Wyrm? Are you sure it was not an illusion?" She asked, fully knowing the tiny creature would have seen through all but the highest level of illusions.

The tiny creature turned indignantly at the pool of bubbling acid still frothing on the floor at their feet, turning back to the mage he simply snarled as if to say 'who is the fool?'

"I must return to the King. I need you to return and not be seen this time. Find me a name Gadrash; we must know who we face. There is great magic in place and I fear it is up to you, my little demon, to find its source. Do this and we can discuss your reduced service contract. How does that sound?" she teased as she commanded him back for what might certainly be a repeat of his last attempt.

As soon as his essence re-gathered in his previous location, he wished himself higher up into the dark sky inside the cavern hovering above the river of lava and the now empty Throne remaining in the twisting nether as to be undetected.. At first he thought himself alone in the chamber, and then he caught movement on his left side. Turning quickly he saw the very large tip of a scaly spiked Dragons tail as it slithered out of the chamber through a giant doorway.

In a blink he reappeared just outside the doorway as it began to slide shut, coming down from inside the top of the rock door way. The Wyrm, either preoccupied by its transformation or perhaps unconcerned by the return of this bothersome Imp, allowed Gad to see it take the form of humanoid, donning the dark hooded robes and walking with the aid of a large black staff.

Knowing his task was incomplete, the tiny Imp willed himself into the smaller chamber the dark one now resided in. Tapestries lined the shinning walls, suits of armor stood along the corridors. Huge chandeliers hung from the vaulted ceiling, large circular holes were open in the tiles allowing the light in when the sun stood high in sky. Gadrash drew up short as the realization struck him. He thought to report to his master just as the words took him.

"If you wish to observe me, pesky Imp, be *confined*." The dark mage had cast his spell while Ish tried to reason out how this could be. His essence screamed against the powerful magic that gripped it and forced it into a magic jar. He had been trapped, and even his master's summons could not retrieve him from this prison. The tiny creature tried several times in vain to break free as his would be capture held out its hand and the shimmering vase floated into it. Smiling a most sinister smile, the creature drew the jar to his face, holding his eye close to the jar blinking several times.

"Whose little pet are you? They must be powerful to have retrieved you so quickly. No matter, at sunrise this will all be unnecessary. I shall deal with your meddling master then."

The mage opened his cloak and dropped the jar into a deep pocket. Gadrash the Impossible had been captured and was helpless to answer the callings of Renna.

CPSIA information can be obtained
at www.ICGtesting.com
Printed in the USA
LVOW10s1215021217
558385LV00026B/1335/P